"I hope you ~~~~~~~~~ **s. I always light a couple before I go to sleep."**

"I don't mind," he replied. Hell yes, he minded the candles that painted her face in beautiful shadows and light. Hell yes, he minded the candles that made the room feel so much smaller and much more intimate.

He walked over to the sofa and found a bed pillow and a soft, hot-pink blanket. He placed his gun on the coffee table, unfolded the blanket and then stretched out.

"Brody?"

"Yeah?" He answered without opening his eyes.

"Somehow, someway I'll make this all up to you."

Visions instantly exploded in his head, erotic visions of the two of them making love. He jerked his head to halt them. "You don't have to make anything up to me."

He couldn't be her friend. She was too much of a temptation and he couldn't be friends with a woman he wanted. He didn't want to be friends with anyone.

He'd see her through this threat and then he had to walk away from her and never look back.

* * *

Be sure to check out the next books in this exciting series:

Cowboys of Holiday Ranch—Where sun, earth and hard work turn men into rugged cowboys…and irresistible heroes!

SHELTERED BY THE COWBOY

BY
CARLA CASSIDY

First Published in Great Britain 2017
By Mills & Boon, an imprint of HarperCollins*Publishers*
1 London Bridge Street, London, SE1 9GF

© 2017 Carla Bracale

ISBN: 978-0-263-93046-7

18-0917

Our policy is to use papers that are natural, renewable and recyclable products and made from wood grown in sustainable forests. The logging and manufacturing processes conform to the legal environmental regulations of the country of origin.

Printed and bound in Spain
by CPI, Barcelona

Carla Cassidy is an award-winning, *New York Times* bestselling author who has written more than one hundred and twenty novels for Mills & Boon. In 1995, she won Best Silhouette Romance from *RT Book Reviews* for *Anything for Danny*. In 1998, she won a Career Achievement Award for Best Innovative Series from *RT Book Reviews*. Carla believes the only thing better than curling up with a good book to read is sitting down at the computer with a good story to write.

Chapter 1

Amanda Wright hummed the tune of "Let It Snow" under her breath as she stamped her feet in an effort to get warm.

The short red Mrs. Santa costume she wore with the white faux fur around the bottom, the neckline and at the cuffs looked cute but did little to provide any real warmth. Wearing flesh-colored tights was almost like being bare-legged, and the short black leather boots on her feet were fashion-forward, but definitely not keeping her toes warm.

She could always step into the small wooden booth's tiny back room, where an oil heater spewed out a bit of warmth, but it was almost time for her to pack it in for the day and she didn't want to miss her last chance to help make a difference.

Darkness had fallen an hour before, and yet the streets of Bitterroot were aglow with the merry lights of the Christmas season. Illuminated red-and-white candy canes hung from every light pole and shoppers still scurried along the sidewalks, trying to get in last-minute supplies before a predicted big snowstorm struck.

Mandy loved this time of year, when the air smelled of evergreen wreaths and cinnamon sticks, and Christmas carols spilled out of every store doorway. Even though the holiday was still a little over two weeks away, Bitterroot was already in the spirit.

She smiled as she saw Butch Cooper approaching the booth. She had dated Butch for about a month and had only recently broken up with him. Thankfully, despite the breakup they had remained good friends.

"Buy a kiss for a dollar," she said. "All proceeds go to the youth program."

Butch pulled his wallet out of his pocket and withdrew a five-dollar bill. "I'll just donate this to the cause," he said and handed her the money.

"Thanks, Butch," she replied. He was such a nice guy, but it hadn't taken her long to realize he wasn't the Prince Charming she was waiting for. Although she'd enjoyed his company, there just hadn't been any real romantic spark with him. "How are you doing?"

"I'm getting by. What about you?"

"The same. I'm keeping busy between the café and this booth," she replied.

"You'd better think about getting yourself home soon," he said. "There's freezing rain moving in and then it's supposed to snow like the devil."

"I'm planning on packing it up in just a little while. I'm hoping to make a little more money before I close down for the night."

"Just don't wait too long. You know Seth wouldn't want you to put yourself at risk for a couple more dollars."

"I know. Thanks, Butch." She watched as the tall, nice-looking cowboy walked away. She released a deep sigh, her breath coming out in a big, frosty puff.

The old saying was that you had to kiss a lot of toads before finally finding a prince. She'd dated most of the single men in town but had yet to find that special toad.

When Seth Richardson had asked her to donate her spare time in a kissing booth for charity, she'd instantly agreed. She knew how important the youth program was in town. She only wished there had been some kind of a youth program when she'd been growing up.

For the past couple of days, when she wasn't working as a waitress at the café, she'd been in this booth. There were two other young women who worked the booth, as well. At least the red-and-white-painted booth was located between the feed store and the mercantile, which meant it got a fair amount of foot traffic.

She stamped her feet once again and mentally cursed the cold. Yes, she loved this time of year and she especially loved to watch it snow, but at the moment, with her fingers and toes half-frozen, she wished it was seventy degrees.

Thoughts of the cold faded away as she saw another handsome cowboy approaching her. The Christmas lights on the buildings flickered and highlighted his strong, bold features in shades of green and red. He was tall and lean, with broad shoulders, and wore his black cowboy hat pulled down as if to warn people away.

Brody Booth.

Just seeing him warmed her a little bit even though they'd scarcely ever exchanged more than a handful of words. He was definitely one sexy cowboy.

"Hey, Brody. How about a kiss for a dollar?" she called out to him. "It's for charity."

He stopped in his tracks and turned to face her. "No, thanks, Mandy. I kind of like being the only man in town you haven't kissed." He turned and continued on his way.

She stared after him in stunned surprise. "You're a jerk, Brody Booth," she called.

His words stung with their implication. She knew her reputation in town was for being fast and loose, a reputation that had begun in high school and had haunted her ever since. Of course, she hadn't helped matters by kissing so many toads.

Brody was one of the best-looking jerks she'd ever seen, but she told herself now that she didn't give two hoots about what he thought of her.

What she'd better start thinking about was getting home. The ping of sleet against the wooden booth was a definite warning that it was time to get out of Dodge.

She closed the awning, stepped into the back space and turned off the heater and the battery-operated light that cast a dim glow. Her coat hung on a small hook next to the back door, and she quickly pulled it on. Then she shoved the small metal money box into her purse, locked up for the night and left the booth.

The sleet stung her face as she hurried to her car. The icy mixture was piling up fast. She probably should have left half an hour before.

The scent of snow whirled on the wind that had picked up, and she was suddenly aware that the streets were virtually deserted.

She hurried to her car and got inside, rubbing her hands together as she waited for the heater to blow hot air. Ice already glazed her windshield, making it impossible for her to see out and drive. Hopefully, between the wipers and the defrost, she could get it cleared off as soon as possible.

Still, by the time she finally crept out of her parking space, the sleet had turned to snow. It wasn't a fluffy, pretty event. Rather, the snowflakes were small and icy and wind-driven.

Visibility was almost nonexistent and the back tires slid each time she tried to accelerate. She was going to be far later getting home than she'd told her father.

Although she lived in a small apartment above the detached garage on the property, when she could she cooked and cleaned for her father.

Of course, he had probably prepared for the snowstorm by buying plenty of liquor. If she was lucky he'd already be passed out by the time she got home. At least she'd thought ahead and had brought home a meatloaf dinner from the café. It sat on the passenger seat in a foam container inside a white bag. When she did get home, if her dad was waiting for her she could have his dinner ready in mere microwave magic minutes.

At the moment his meal wasn't her concern. Just getting home in this mess was her main issue. The snowflakes were now bigger, but coming down at an alarming pace. Her muscles tensed as she hunched over the steering wheel and squinted to see the road ahead.

She hadn't even made it out of town when she felt the disheartening slide of her tires against the pavement. The car was moving sideways. Frantically she turned the wheel first left and then right to straighten out. In horror she realized she was no longer in control.

She knew better than to apply the brakes, but she was sliding on pure ice and headed for a ditch. Her heart hitched in her chest and she braced.

She squealed as the car hit the ditch and came to a dead stop. She tried to move forward and the tires spun impotently. She threw it into Reverse with the same results.

"Darn, darn!" She hit the steering wheel with her palms. She was good and stuck.

She'd have to call for a tow. She unfastened her seat belt and pulled her purse onto her lap, rummaging around inside it until she grabbed her cell phone.

Before she could dial a number, she glanced in her rearview mirror and gasped in renewed horror. Twin headlights were careening toward the back of her car, and she couldn't move out of the way. *Objects in this mirror are closer than they appear.* She read the words on her passenger mirror just before she squeezed her eyes tightly closed.

Bracing once again, she expected a crash, but it was more like a hard bump. The pickup truck hit her hard enough to throw the meatloaf dinner off the passenger seat and onto the floor, but thankfully not hard enough to injure her.

She looked in her rearview mirror once again and saw Brody getting out of the truck that had hit her.

Great, just what she needed to make a bad situation even worse.

She rolled down her window and heard his muttered curses as he made his way to her driver side. "Sorry," he said. "That patch of road is pure ice. Are you okay?"

"Tell me about it. I didn't exactly drive into this ditch on purpose," she replied drily. "And I'm fine, but frustrated."

"It looks like I'm going to owe you a bumper."

"Right now I'm not worried about a bumper. What I need is a tow out of this ditch."

"That makes two of us. Mind if I get in?" He gestured to the passenger seat.

"Knock yourself out," she replied. She rolled up her window as he left the driver side and walked around the front of the car to get into the passenger seat.

"What's this?" he asked as he maneuvered his feet so he didn't step on the bag on the floor. Once he was in, he moved the seat back to accommodate the length of his legs.

"Oh yeah, you owe me a bumper and a meatloaf special from the café," she replied.

He filled the small interior of the car with the scent of the outdoors mingling with a woodsy cologne. Snow clung to his slightly shaggy dark hair and sinfully long dark eyelashes. He also wore the same frown she always saw on his face.

"I'll call for a tow truck and we'll worry about the bumper and meatloaf dinner later. The snow is really starting to pile up." He pulled his cell phone from his pocket and punched in a series of numbers.

"Larry, it's Brody Booth. Amanda Wright and I are stuck in a ditch just past the turnoff to the motel. We need a tow."

It was obvious by his deepening frown that he wasn't happy with whatever he was hearing, and a ball of anxiety unfurled in her chest.

"Okay, I understand. Yeah, I'll be waiting for your call." He hung up and pocketed his phone. "Larry and every other tow person in town is busy working the highway, which he said looks like a skating rink, so basically we're on our own."

"On our own?" She echoed his words as she stared at him in horror. "For how long?"

"It might be morning before somebody can finally get to us."

"Morning? We can't stay out here all night. I don't even have a blanket in the car," she said.

"You're right. We can't," he agreed. "I suggest we walk to the motel. We can get rooms for the night and be out here first thing in the morning when help finally comes."

She stared over her shoulder, where the motel sign blinked faintly like a red heartbeat through the haze of the falling snow. The snow. A shiver swept over her. It was deep enough now that it would swallow her little boots with the first step.

"Do you have some pants you can put on?" Brody asked. Was there a slight hint of disdain in his voice or was she only imagining it?

"Nope, just these sexy flesh-tone tights," she replied flippantly. "Don't worry about me, Brody. I'm used to taking care of myself." She buttoned up her coat and mentally prepared for the cold trek to the motel.

"Wait for me. I need to lock up my truck." He left the car and a gust of frigid air blew in.

She should have left the booth earlier. She should have been smart enough to keep a survival bag with blankets and bottled water and protein bars in the car. Sometimes she could be so stupid.

It didn't take long for Brody to come back. He pulled open the driver's door, and precariously she stepped out of the car. The icy wind instantly stole her breath, and she slid unsteadily with her first step.

He must have noticed because he grabbed her firmly by the upper arm, and together they made their way out of the ditch and back to the road.

It was impossible to speak with the howling wind in her ears and the driving snow hitting her in the face. She was just grateful for Brody's strength as she slipped more than once and would have landed on her face or her butt if he hadn't steadied her.

She was an icicle, frozen from the top of her head to the tips of her toes. All she could think about was a nice warm room, a very hot shower and then a bed to snuggle down in to wait out the storm.

She might have sobbed in relief when they reached the motel office but she was too frozen to cry. Brody immediately released his hold on her as he greeted Fred Ferguson, the owner of the motel.

"Heck of a night," Fred said, his gaze behind his dark-rimmed glasses drifting from Brody to Mandy.

"The road is definitely treacherous tonight," Brody replied.

"So are you both stuck?"

"Yeah, we're both in a ditch down the road. We each need a room for the night," Brody replied.

"That's going to be a problem," Fred replied.

Every frozen muscle in her body tensed. What now? "A p-p-problem?" she managed to stutter through her chattering teeth.

Fred nodded. "I've only got one room left."

Brody visibly stiffened. "Only one?"

A wave of dread swept through Mandy. Apparently she would be spending the night with a man who didn't like her and definitely didn't respect her. Could this night get any worse?

"A double?" Brody asked hopefully.

"Nope, it's a single with a queen bed."

The night just got worse. She watched, dumbfounded, as Brody slowly pulled his wallet out of his pocket and released a deep, audible sigh. "I guess we'll take it."

Brody had had a long, rough day and the idea of being locked in a motel room with the voluptuous, beautiful Mandy Wright was a candle on the top of a crap cake.

He grabbed the key Fred placed on the counter and then headed out the door with Mandy trailing just behind him. There was no way he was going to crawl into bed with her tonight. Hopefully there would be a comfy chair in the room where he could sprawl until morning.

He had a feeling if he found himself under the sheets with Mandy, something would happen and they would wind up having sex, and he refused to be another cowboy she'd bedded and then tossed aside.

At room four he unlocked the door and opened it, reached inside to turn on the overhead light and then stepped aside so she could go in before him. She walked into the center of the room and turned to face him.

Her full lips were blue and her dark hair hung in wet strands around her shoulders. She shivered uncontrollably, and he shut the door more forcefully than he intended. "Go get in a hot shower," he commanded. "You're soaking wet."

"But... I... I don't have anything else to put on," she replied, her lips barely moving.

Brody frowned, then walked over to the bed and yanked off the blue-and-gray spread. "Use this to wrap up in until your clothes can dry." He thrust it into her arms.

As she turned and disappeared into the bathroom, he released another deep sigh. He shrugged out of his own coat and then turned up the heat in the room.

The room was one of the smaller ones the motel had to offer, and the chair, which he'd hoped would be big and comfortable enough for a night's sleep, wasn't. It was a spindly straight-backed chair in front of the window that would assure no sleep at all for the night.

He held his hands over the heat that had begun to blow from a vent. He could still smell her, a scent of brown sugar and vanilla that was intensely appealing.

At the sound of the shower running, he tried hard not to visualize a naked Mandy. Far too often in the past he'd fantasized about a naked Mandy. Jeez, this was going to be tough.

A glance out the window showed him that the snow was still coming down. The snow wasn't so bad, but the icy mixture that had preceded it would have the whole town at a standstill.

He sat down on the edge of the chair and pulled off his boots. The bottoms of his jeans legs were wet, but there was no way in hell he intended to strip down. It was bad enough that Mandy was going to wear only a bedspread when she got out of the bathroom. A wave of warmth swept through him at the very thought.

Of all the women in town he could have been snowbound with, why did it have to be the one woman he was attracted to? A woman who, rumor had it, ate men for breakfast and spit them out by dinner? Not that he would care. He didn't ever want a relationship with a woman.

At least she hadn't moaned and groaned on the miserable trek to the motel. She'd soldiered up, lowered her head and had done what needed to be done without a single complaint, although she had to have been miserable.

He looked at his watch. It was just six thirty. What were they going to do to pass the rest of the evening? His stomach growled and he almost wished he'd picked up that meatloaf dinner from the floorboard and brought it to the room. He'd not only skipped dinner but also missed lunch. He wondered if she'd eaten dinner.

Maybe he'd check out the motel vending machines and see if he could grab something there. With that thought in mind he pulled his boots on once again.

A vision of Mandy clad in a red, white and blue sparkly bra exploded in his mind. It wasn't just a fantasy. It was what she'd worn at the Holiday Ranch barn dance the month before. She'd been a sizzling sight as she'd danced and laughed and stirred something inside him that had been dormant for years... desire.

It had been a costume party and she'd come as a patriot, and since that night he'd had a hard time getting her out of his head.

As the sound of the shower stopped, his entire body tensed with an uncharacteristic anxiety. He quickly moved back to the chair and picked up the television remote from the table. She'd be coming out of the bathroom at any minute. At least the television would provide a welcome distraction from her. He punched the on button and stared at the message that danced across the screen.

No Signal Detected.

The bathroom door opened and she walked out, a vision wrapped in a bedspread.

This was definitely going to be a long night.

Chapter 2

The hot shower had been heavenly. Of course, she would have liked to have her own shower gel and a hair dryer and all the comforts of home, but she'd been grateful that her purse had contained a hair brush, lip gloss and a little bottle of her favorite body spray.

She wrapped the spread around her like an oversized towel, leaving her shoulders bare, but hiding anything that shouldn't be shown.

Of all the men in the town, why did she have to be stuck here with Brody? The other women at the café called him the brooding one. He might be hot and handsome, but he didn't seem to possess a glimmer of a sense of humor or even the ability to smile...at least, not at her.

Still, she'd been oddly attracted to him for a long time, despite his stern countenance and the fact that she felt like he somehow judged her and found her lacking.

Her heart beat just a little more quickly than usual when she walked out of the bathroom. He looked at her, and for just a moment, as his gaze slowly swept up and down her, she felt completely naked.

"The television isn't working," he said and stood, his gaze shifting to some point over her right shoulder. "I don't know about you, but I'm going to get hungry before this night is over. I'll check out the vending machines. Do you want something?"

"Whatever you can get. I haven't eaten since just before noon," she replied.

He pulled on his coat and flew out the door as if the very devil himself was chasing him. Mandy drew a deep breath and sat on the edge of the bed. This whole situation was definitely awkward and would probably only get more so as the night wore on.

She jumped up, went into the bathroom, grabbed her wet Santa costume and carried it into the main room. She draped it and her wet tights over one of the heater vents.

Maybe she and Brody both could relax better once her clothes were dry and she was dressed again. They just had to make the best of things for the night.

Instead of sitting on the edge of the mattress, she plumped up the pillows on what she decided was going to be her side and then stretched out.

She considered calling her father to tell him she was stuck for the night, but then decided against it. The last thing she needed right now was for him to tell her she was stupid and a huge disappointment to him. She'd heard that song from him enough times to last the rest of her life.

Besides, when she didn't make it home, surely he would realize she might be stuck somewhere. The last thing George Wright would ever think to do was worry about his only daughter.

She tensed as Brody came back into the room, his shoulders and hair once again snow-covered. "I got one of everything the vending machine offered. I figured we can each pick what we want." He set two sodas on the dresser and then began pulling goodies out of his coat pockets. "I hope you like cola."

"Cola is fine...thanks," she replied.

By the time they finished picking at the snacks, Mandy had scored a chocolate cupcake, a bag of corn chips, roasted peanuts and a cherry pie. She placed all the goodies and one of the sodas on the nightstand next to her and then patted the other side of the bed.

"You might as well get comfortable and relax, Brody," she said. "It's going to be a long night."

He scowled and placed his snacks on the other nightstand. He then shrugged off his coat, pulled off his boots and stretched out next to her on the very edge of the bed.

"If you take a deep breath you're going to fall right off the side," she said.

"I'm fine," he replied curtly.

She propped herself up on one elbow to face him. "Are you going to be in a bad mood the whole night?"

He looked at her in surprise. "What makes you think I'm in a bad mood?"

"Gee, I don't know. Since you scowl all the time, it's hard to tell when you're in a good mood." She consciously ignored the crazy warmth that swept through her at his nearness. His body heat radiated toward her and the scent of him was so pleasant.

"I've just been thinking about all the things I should be doing around the ranch. I'm acting as foreman right now and I should be there." He leaned over and grabbed a package of potato chips off his nightstand.

Mandy knew Brody worked on the Holiday Ranch, and the local gossipmongers had been buzzing about everything that had taken place there over the past month.

"I still can't believe Adam Benson killed all those people," she said. "He seemed like such a nice guy... always with a pleasant smile," she said pointedly.

Seven unsolved murders had taken place on the Holiday Ranch fifteen years ago and Chief of Police Dillon Bowie had been determined to solve the crime. It wasn't until ranch foreman Adam tried to kill ranch owner Cassie Peterson that Dillon was finally able to solve the crimes and make sure Adam would never hurt anyone again. Adam had been killed when Dillon saved Cassie. Since then, Dillon had moved in with Cassie, and there was talk about a wedding in the near future.

"All of us were surprised. None of us had any clue how dangerous and sick Adam was." He ripped open the bag of chips and offered it to her.

"So, you're now the new foreman there." She plucked out a chip and popped it into her mouth. It was vaguely irritating to her that he hadn't really looked at her since he'd returned to the room with the goodies.

"Temporarily," he replied. "Cassie offered me the position, and I took it for now with the understanding that I might not be the best man for the job."

"Other than your obvious lack of people skills, why wouldn't you be the best man for the job?"

"I do fine with most people," he replied with a touch of irritation.

"So then it's just me you don't want to be nice to."

He finally really looked at her, his dark brown eyes perfectly matching the brown in his plaid flannel shirt. Dear heaven, the man was so hot. His broad shoulders filled his side of the bed and his jeans fit tight on his slim hips, flat abdomen and long legs.

"Mandy, I don't really know you."

"Then tonight is a perfect opportunity for us to get to know each other better. Maybe we could even walk out of here in the morning as friends. I could always use a new friend. I don't have many."

"And why is that?" He gazed at her curiously.

Warmth swept into her cheeks. "I'm sure you know why most women don't like me. With my reputation, I wouldn't like me, either." There, she'd mentioned the elephant in the room.

"Your reputation?"

She released a small, slightly bitter laugh. "Don't play dumb with me, Brody Booth. I know what people say about me behind my back, that I'm fast and loose and wild, but you shouldn't believe everything you hear."

"I'm just wondering how Butch Cooper is going to feel in the morning when word gets out that we spent the night together." He returned his gaze to some point just over her shoulder.

"Butch is old news. We broke up soon after Cassie's barn dance. I'm not seeing anyone right now. What about you? Is somebody going to be upset with you about tonight?" She'd never heard anything about his personal life.

"I don't have anyone in my life and I don't want anyone."

"And why is that?" she asked curiously. "Don't you want to get married and eventually have kids?"

"Nope."

"Are you gay?"

He released a small laugh. "Nope."

For a moment she couldn't remember what they'd just been talking about. All she could think of was that low, slightly husky and very sexy sound that had escaped him. She turned and grabbed her corn chips off the nightstand and then faced him once again.

"Why do you date so many men?" he asked.

She looked at him in surprise. "I'm twenty-nine years old, I'm single and I'm looking for the toad who will become my Prince Charming. So far, they've all just been common toads."

"Maybe your standards are too high," he replied. Once again he wasn't looking at her but rather peering someplace over her head.

"Probably," she agreed easily. "But why would I lower my standards as to who I want to spend the rest of my life with? I want a man who loves me desperately, somebody who will always have my back no matter what. I've never, ever had anyone like that in my entire life."

"What about your family?"

She masked that particular pain with a small laugh. "My mother died when I was ten. A month after her death, my older brother ran away and never came back. My father pretty much hates my existence and only keeps me around so I can cook and clean for him."

Afraid that she had sounded too harsh about her

father, she continued, "Dad hurt his back nine years ago and had to go on disability, and he never got over my mother's death. He needs my help and I'm glad to do it. All I want is to be good enough that he'll be proud of me and love me."

Jeez, what was she doing baring her soul to him? She really didn't know him at all. She grabbed a chip from her bag, not wanting to think about how alone she'd felt for most of her life.

"You never heard from your brother again?" he asked.

She shook her head. "When Graham left he never looked back. I think maybe it helped break my father's heart even more and that's what made him so hard and bitter. So, what about you? What's your family story?" She didn't want to think about her brother or her father anymore. It hurt too much.

He stared up at the ceiling, as if contemplating whether to share anything with her or not. "You've probably heard that all of us cowboys at the Holiday Ranch were throwaway kids. Cass Holiday took us in when we were all in our early teens."

"Everyone in town has heard the story," she replied.

"I was fourteen when my father threw me out of the house because he caught me smoking a cigarette. It was almost a relief to be forced to leave. Like you, I lost my mama when I was young. My father was a brutal man with an uncontrollable rage inside him and that rage was usually focused on me."

He turned to look at her, his eyes dark and unreadable. "I was fairly lucky. I'd only been out on the streets about a month when Francine Rogers, a social worker who was friends with Cass, offered me the chance to work on a ranch and brought me to Cass."

"I didn't know Cass well before she died, although I've heard all kinds of wild stories about her."

His lips curled up in a beautiful smile that stole her breath away. "She was quite a character…tough as nails, yet she made all of us feel valued and wanted. Most of us probably would have died on the streets if not for her."

"It's so nice she gave you all a second chance."

"She gave us hope and while we were all a little worried when Cassie, her niece, took over, everything has been different, but fine."

Mandy released a small sigh. "I'm hoping someday I can get to a really good place with my father."

Brody's smile disappeared. "And what if that doesn't happen?" he asked.

"Then I'll just have to be content with the knowledge that I did everything I could for him," she said with more assurance than she felt. "See?" she added with a wide grin. "We're getting along just fine. We have a lot in common."

He quirked a dark eyebrow upward. "Bad childhoods don't necessarily make us good friend material."

She wasn't sure why it was so important to her, but she wanted him to come away from this night seeing her as so much more than her crummy reputation.

"Do you like pizza?" she asked.

"Who doesn't?" he replied easily.

"What about Mexican food?"

"There isn't much I don't like to eat," he said.

"That's great. You like to eat and I love to cook. That's something else that makes us potential friend material."

For the next couple of hours they talked about all kinds of topics. They both enjoyed country and western music and disliked hard rock. Autumn was her favorite season and he liked spring the best. The more time that passed with light conversation, the more they relaxed with each other.

She told him about her dream to someday open a little restaurant of her own, and he talked about his life and work on the ranch. But she knew her attraction to him would go nowhere. He didn't seem to be drawn to her in that way at all.

They had just finished eating all their goodies when the conversation returned to her reputation.

"You didn't go to Bitterroot High School," she said.

"No, Cass decided it was best to homeschool all of us."

"You were lucky. It was a seething pool of gossip and drama, and that's when my bad reputation started. I was dating Richard Herridge when we were both juniors. He was on the football team and real popular."

"He works on the Humes ranch now," Brody said, his scowl back.

"He's just another creep like all the rest of the men who work for Humes," she replied. The Holiday Ranch hands and the Humes men didn't get along. The entire town knew about the ongoing feud between the neighboring ranches.

"Anyway, we'd been dating for about a month and he started pressuring me to have sex with him. I finally said it wasn't going to happen and I broke up with him. The next morning everyone at school was talking about how I had sex with him, and then he broke up with me because he'd gotten what he wanted. And that's when it all began."

She couldn't begin to speak of the depth of the anguish that had chased her through the last of her high school years. Girls scorned her and lots of the boys dated her and then lied about having sex with her.

Even now there were women who were reluctant to have anything to do with her, but her dance card was always filled. She'd never figured out a way to change people's perception of her, and she'd finally stopped trying long ago.

"You haven't exactly gone out of your way to try to change people's view of you," Brody said.

"What's the point? People expect provocative behavior from me and so that's what I give them. I'm kind of like a cow that has been branded, and once that brand is done there's no way to get rid of it."

She shrugged and then grabbed at the bedspread before it could slip downward. "Every town needs a bad girl and I guess I play that role in Bitterroot."

He gazed at her for a long moment and then released a deep sigh. "It's getting late. I suggest we both get some sleep. Hopefully the tow trucks will be out here early in the morning."

"My clothes should be dry by now." She got up from the bed, careful to keep the bedspread in place, and grabbed her clothing from the heater vent. "I'll be right back."

It took her only minutes in the bathroom to redress in the now warm and dry Santa costume. When she returned to the room, together they put the bedspread back on. Then he turned out the light and they got into bed. She snuggled under the covers and he remained on top.

Even in the dark she was acutely aware of him so close to her, close enough that she could swear she heard the steady beat of his heart. It was slightly thrilling even though she knew it shouldn't be so.

"Brody?"

"Yeah?"

"Thanks for being so nice to me tonight."

"Go to sleep, Mandy."

"Okay." She turned over and tried not to think about how much she wished that he would pull her into his arms, hold her for just a little while against his broad chest until she drifted off to happy dreams.

But if they walked out of here tomorrow morning and could be real friends, she'd be happy with that... because she suspected she'd have to be.

Something tickled at his nose. Something...fuzzy. No...furry. Brody opened his eyes to early morning light seeping in around the edges of the blue draperies at the window. Mandy's fur collar was right under his nose and he was spooned around the back of her as if he belonged there.

Move, a small inner voice urged him, but he ignored it. For just a brief moment he remained perfectly still, enjoying the sensation of a warm, shapely female in his arms. It was a rare moment for him as it had been a very long time since he'd been in a position to hold a woman.

Amanda Wright was nothing like he had expected her to be. He wasn't sure what he'd expected, but she'd been far more likeable and with a soft vulnerability that had surprised him. She was more like a beautiful playful puppy dog than a femme fatale.

Was her reputation overblown? Possibly. It was easy to be labeled in a small town, although she'd admitted she could be provocative in keeping with her role as the bad girl.

It had been obvious she loved her father and longed for a better relationship with him. A tight ball of tension filled his chest as he thought of his own father.

It had been Cass who had tried to make him understand that his father's brutality and inability to love was his fault and not Brody's. Still, Brody knew himself to be dangerous damaged goods, and that was why he would never marry or have children. He was a bad risk for any woman.

A distant growl of a snowblower replaced the silence of the room. He quickly rolled away from Mandy and stood, grateful that she didn't awaken.

The last thing he wanted her to know was that in sleep he had cuddled with her. It had been bad enough last night when they'd talked and he'd tried so hard to keep his gaze away from her creamy naked shoulders and the spill of her long, dark, slightly wavy hair. He'd been on a slow burn for most of the night.

He raked a hand through his hair and walked over to the window. Moving one of the heavy blue curtains aside just a bit, he peered out.

The sun shone bright on the snow that had fallen the night before. There was less snow than he'd anticipated. Still, the ground was covered by about three to four inches of the white stuff.

Fred Ferguson manned the snowblower and was in the process of clearing off the walkways. Hopefully it wouldn't be too long before Larry Jerrod called to say his team was on their way to pull Mandy and him out of the ditch.

In the meantime there was a coffee machine next to the sink and he definitely needed a jolt of caffeine to clear his head. Within minutes the scent of the fresh brew filled the room.

He'd just poured himself a cup and sat in the spindly chair near the window when Mandy stirred. She stretched like a contented kitten and then offered him a sleepy smile. "We survived," she said, her voice slightly husky.

"We did," he agreed. He stood and opened the curtains, hoping to get her out of the bed. She was far too much of a temptation in the bed, wearing that damned Santa costume that showcased her full breasts, small waist and long, shapely legs.

He heard the rustle of the sheets, and when he turned back around she was up and at the sink, pouring herself a cup of coffee. Hell, she was a temptation out of bed, as well.

She walked over and joined him at the window. "It looks a lot better out there this morning than it did last night."

"I'm hoping it won't be long before we can get on our way."

"I'm sure you're anxious to get back to the ranch.

Thank goodness today is my day off at the café so all I have to do is get home." A tiny frown danced across her forehead. "I guess I should probably call my dad."

She set her cup down, went over to the nightstand and dug in her purse. She retrieved her cell phone and then sat on the edge of the bed and punched in numbers. She turned slightly to face away from him. "Dad, it's me. I just wanted to let you know that I'm waiting for a tow. I slid into a ditch last night and had to stay at the motel."

Brody wasn't trying to listen in, but although he couldn't make out her father's specific words, he certainly heard the loud, rough tone.

"Yeah, Dad, I know it was stupid of me to wind up in a ditch and I'm sorry you had to make your own dinner last night. I'll make it all up to you when I get home. I'll fix you a terrific breakfast."

Apparently her father hung up on her. She dropped her phone back into the depths of her purse and then turned and gave Brody a sheepish smile. "He isn't much of a morning person."

Brody had a feeling George Wright wasn't much of a noon or night person, either. From what little gossip he'd heard about George, the man was a drunk who had more enemies than he had friends.

"What are you planning to make for breakfast?" he asked in an attempt to lighten the mood.

Her thick-lashed, caramel-colored eyes took on

a sparkle and her lips curved into a smile. "I make this great peach French toast casserole with pecans and lots of cream and spices."

"Hmm, sounds good."

"Want to come over for breakfast?" she asked eagerly. "You know, just as a friend."

Brody cast his gaze back out the window. "I don't think this morning would be a good time."

"Well, of course it wouldn't," she replied agreeably. "I can be such a dunce sometimes."

At that moment Brody's phone rang. It was Larry telling him that he'd be at their cars within fifteen minutes. When the brief call ended they both abandoned their coffee cups for their coats and then stepped outside for the trek to their vehicles.

"Whew, it's still cold out here," Mandy said and pulled her coat collar up closer around her neck.

"Wait here," Brody told her. "I'll be right back." Before they left here there was one thing he wanted to do. He approached Fred Ferguson, who cut the engine on the snowblower.

"You taking off?" he asked.

"We are," Brody replied. "I just wanted to tell you that if I hear any gossip about Mandy and me spending the night together I'll hold you personally responsible."

"You know I'm not a gossip," Fred blustered, his eyes wide behind his dark-rimmed glasses.

Brody knew no such thing. In fact, Fred loved to

indulge himself in juicy gossip. "I'm just giving you a heads-up." As he returned to Mandy, the snow-blower roared back to life. The last thing he wanted was for the night to further stain Mandy's reputation.

"Ready?" he asked Mandy when he reached her.

"Ready," she replied.

The ground was still slippery and Mandy's little boots were about as useful as a pig in a poker game. He took her by the arm and she leaned into him as they trudged forward.

When they finally reached her car, he released his hold on her. She peered up at him. "All's well that ends well, right?"

"Right," he agreed easily.

"Thank you, Brody."

"For what?"

Those winsome eyes of hers gazed at him intently. "Thank you for being nice to me and for being such a gentleman."

Thank God she hadn't been privy to his lustful thoughts throughout their time together. "It was no problem," he replied easily.

Once again her eyes sparkled with liveliness. "Hey, maybe we should exchange phone numbers. It would be nice to be able to talk to each other oc-casionally."

He couldn't very well say no to her, not with her lips curved into such a wide smile, not with her eyes gleaming so brightly. It took only a minute for them to put their numbers into each other's cell phones, and then he encouraged her to get into her car and warm it up.

He climbed into his truck and looked down at her number in his phone. Would he ever call her? It was doubtful. She was a temptation he definitely didn't need in his life.

He was just grateful their night together was over and he could get back to his solitary life, where he could work hard and sleep without dreams.

Since Cass had died in the spring storm, there was really only one woman he now believed in, and he saw her about once a week. He trusted her with the secret that had haunted him for years, and she was the only woman he'd ever allow to have a place in his life.

Chapter 3

"Hey, handsome," Mandy greeted Sawyer Quincy with a smile. The copper-haired cowboy was from the Holiday Ranch. "What are you doing in here for lunch all by yourself?"

He swept off his brown cowboy hat and placed it on his lap. "I came in to pick up some supplies and got a hankering for some of Daisy's chicken noodle soup," he replied. "How are you doing, Mandy?"

"Good, especially since some of the snow has finally melted. I'm getting off early today and I'm planning on spending the whole evening drifting from store to store and doing some Christmas shopping."

"That sounds like fun for you," he replied.

"How about a couple of thick slices of Daisy's homemade bread with butter to go along with that soup?" she asked.

"That sounds great...and a cup of coffee."

"Got it," Mandy wrote on the order pad and then turned to head to the kitchen pass to turn in the ticket.

It had been three days since the overnight snowstorm, and during those days the temperatures had crept above freezing and the sun had shone, making muddy soup out of the snow and ice.

The café was busy. It was as if everyone in Bitterroot had decided it was time to get out of their house to have lunch.

She placed the ticket, poured Sawyer his coffee and then turned in time to see Fred Ferguson being seated at one of her tables. He offered her a small scowl as she approached the table.

"Afternoon, Fred," she greeted him brightly. "What can I start you off with to drink?"

"Before I order anything, I just want to say I didn't appreciate your boyfriend threatening me the other morning."

She looked at him in surprise. "Brody? He isn't my boyfriend, and what did he threaten you about?"

"He told me if he heard any idle gossip about you and him being in that room together for the night he'd consider me personally responsible. I don't gossip about what goes on in my motel and I definitely don't need a big, burly cowboy trying to intimidate me. Now, I'd like to start off with a cup of coffee and then I'll take the special of the day."

"Got it," Mandy replied. She left the table with her thoughts whirling. Why had Brody talked to Fred about keeping their night together a secret?

Had he been trying to somehow protect her reputation? That was almost laughable. Maybe he'd been attempting to protect his own.

This thought hurt more than a little bit, especially considering the fact that the night before she'd called him just to chat for a few minutes and they'd wound up talking for almost half an hour.

It had been nice to have the sound of his deep voice still ringing in her head when she'd finally drifted off to sleep. She now shoved thoughts of Brody away as she hurried to deliver food and take more orders.

She'd worked as a bank clerk until just after Cassie's barn party. She suspected she'd been let go because she'd worn a red, white and blue sparkly bra to the party. It had been a costume party and she'd gone as a patriot superheroine. The president of the bank, Margery Martin, had not found it amusing.

Mandy's termination had wound up being a godsend. She belonged working with food. Right now she just delivered it up, but she was hoping she could work her way up to Daisy allowing her to be in the kitchen and then one day owning her own place.

She put every tip in jelly jars under her bed and hoped eventually to have enough to start her own restaurant. What she envisioned wouldn't compete with Daisy's café. She'd like to open another café, but knew the competition with Daisy wouldn't be good. She might decide to open a restaurant that offered more of a fine dining experience.

A dream. That was all it was right now, along with her dream of eventually finding her prince. In the meantime there were orders to be taken and diners to be served.

It was just after six when she went into the back room and took off her apron. She was looking forward to an evening of wandering through the stores and looking at Christmas goodies.

Since her phone call with Brody the night before, she'd wondered what might be good friend etiquette. Would it be too forward for her to buy him a little gift? And if she did, what on earth would it be?

She pulled on her coat, left the back room and headed toward the café's front door. "Don't spend too much money on a Christmas gift for me," Daisy said with amusement. "I've got everything I want except a husband and I'm not sure I want another one of those."

Mandy laughed. "I'll keep that in mind," she replied. "I'll see you at eleven tomorrow."

"Enjoy your night," Daisy called after her.

Mandy left the café. It had been an exhausting day and her feet were killing her, but the cold night air and the sight of the cheery red and green lights filled her with a new burst of energy.

It would be nice to have company while she shopped, but she was accustomed to being alone when she wasn't dating anyone. At the moment she didn't even feel like dating.

At least she'd taken care of her father's dinner. Last night she'd made chicken and dumplings and there had been enough leftovers for him to warm himself up a plate this evening.

She had nothing on her mind as she headed for the mercantile store. She went inside, and a bell tinkled merrily overhead. The store smelled of spiced apple candles and evergreens and a variety of scents that spoke of the holiday. She drew in a deep breath. Christmas carols played softly from someplace overhead and Mandy was immersed in the holiday.

The mercantile store always dedicated shelf space not only for Christmas decorations but also for all kinds of gift sets and items that never appeared any other time of year.

She knew her father wouldn't buy her anything. He even refused to have a tree put up in his house. But tonight Mandy intended to go home to her own apartment and put up and decorate the three-foot tabletop tree she'd gotten a couple of years ago.

She always bought a Christmas present for her mother and her brother. She'd wrap them and put them under her tree, and then a couple of days before Christmas she donated them to charity.

While they were under her tree she'd remember her love for her mother and her older brother, and she'd mourn the fact that her family had fallen apart when Regina Wright had passed away after battling cancer.

She rounded an aisle with her shopping cart and nearly bumped into Dillon Bowie and Cassie Peterson. "Hey, guys. Christmas shopping?"

"Just getting some ideas," Cassie replied. She leaned into Dillon with a happy smile. "He won't tell me what he wants, so I'm trying to find out if anything we see sparks his interest."

"So far she's told me at least a dozen things that she'd like to have," Dillon replied with a teasing grin at the petite blonde next to him. "Besides, I keep telling her that I've got all I want. I have her."

"Ah, that's so sweet," Mandy replied. Dillon and Cassie were the newest happy couple in Bitterroot. Through all the drama that had taken place at the Holiday Ranch, they had come together in love. Mandy thought it was all wildly romantic.

"Thank goodness most of the snow is gone," Cassie said.

"It definitely makes it easier to get around," Mandy replied.

"How's the kissing booth going?" Cassie asked.

"I think once it's over Seth is going to be pleased with the money raised," Mandy replied. "We have some generous people in this town."

"Bitterroot has always been a charitable town," Cassie agreed.

The three of them visited for just a few more minutes and then Mandy continued her quest for perfect Christmas gifts. By the time she made her way home, she'd bought a beautiful eternity scarf for her mother, a bottle of cologne for her brother and a black leather wallet for her father. He'd probably hate it, but at least she'd tried.

She'd also picked up a pair of earrings in the shape of reindeer that lit up for Daisy. The flamboyant café owner would get a hoot out of them. With Mandy's packages in a large shopping bag, she headed home.

The studio apartment above the detached garage had originally been rented out to make extra money, but four years ago the last tenant had moved out and Mandy had convinced her father to rent it to her.

It wasn't huge, but there was a living room space with a sofa, a chair and a small kitchenette. There was still enough room left over for her queen-size bed shoved against a wall, a dresser and the bathroom.

The Wright ranch was relatively large, with lots of good pasture and a wooded area with beautiful shade trees. But it had been years since her father had actually worked the ranch. Now he preferred either sitting in his recliner and complaining about his life, or heading to the Watering Hole, where he could try to drink away those complaints.

As she prepared to wrap the silky scarf in shiny silver paper, her thoughts turned to her mother. Mandy had only a few memories of the woman who had given birth to her, and all of them were pleasant ones. Her mother had loved music and often sang as she cleaned or cooked. She had also been a beautiful woman and Mandy had been told by people in town that she looked just like her.

Her brother, Graham, had been a terrific big brother until the day he'd left. At first she'd thought he'd come back to get her, but she'd given up on that belief years ago.

By nine o'clock the tree was up on a small table in the living room area and all the presents were wrapped and under the tree. She sat on the sofa for a few minutes and admired the way the little white lights shone on the silver-and-red ornaments.

Christmas could be a little depressing for her since most of the time she celebrated alone. But she always tried to focus on positive things to keep the blues away.

With the tree up and the presents wrapped, she ate a chicken salad sandwich and changed into her pajamas. Finally she got into bed with her cell phone and considered calling Brody.

It would be nice to end the pleasant night as she had the night before, with Brody's deep voice the last sound she heard before falling asleep. She decided not to call him. She didn't want to seem too forward and wind up pushing him away.

She slept without dreams and awakened to the sound of her alarm. It was six fifteen. She would have loved to linger in bed, but her father was usually an early riser and liked his breakfast around seven.

She showered and dressed in the yellow T-shirt and black slacks that were her café uniform, then grabbed her purse and headed toward the big two-story house in the distance.

Over the past couple of years she'd tried to convince her father to sell the ranch and move closer to town. He didn't need the land or the huge house, but he'd refused to consider it. She'd thought about moving into an apartment in town but knew her father depended on her rent money to help pay the bills.

The eastern sky was just starting to light as she unlocked the back door and stepped into the large kitchen. The sound of the television drifting in from the living room let her know her father was already up.

She shrugged off her coat and hung it on the back of a chair at the table, then moved to the coffee maker on the counter. Before greeting him she needed to get the coffee going. George Wright without his morning coffee was definitely an irritable bear.

As she waited, she looked around the kitchen, remembering the old days when they sat at the table as a family, the old days when her mother had been alive and Graham had been home.

When there was enough fresh brew, she filled a cup and left the kitchen. "Morning, Dad," she said cheerfully as she entered the living room.

She could see the back of his head above the black leather recliner chair that faced the television, but he didn't answer her.

Great, he wasn't speaking to her...again. He was probably mad at her for going shopping the night before and leaving him to warm up his own dinner.

"Dad?" She rounded the chair and froze in horror.

Her father's brown eyes stared blankly forward. His slashed throat gaped wide and blood had splashed down the front of him. There was no question that he was dead.

"No." The cup of coffee slipped from her hand and crashed to the hardwood floor as a scream released from her.

Brody lingered over a cup of coffee in the cowboy dining room, listening as Sawyer and Mac McBride discussed the weather and the forecast for a dryer winter than usual.

If it had been springtime the men would already be out of here and doing morning chores in the field, but in winter the schedule was far more lax.

Aside from providing feed and water for the cattle and taking care of the horses, they spent most of their time repairing and maintaining equipment.

He tuned out their conversation and instead found himself thinking about Mandy. He'd been surprised when she'd called him two nights before just to chat. Brody didn't just "chat" with anyone, but he'd found it impossible to remain stoic and distant with her. She was so bubbly and happy, and he found her remarkably easy to talk to.

They'd discussed the people they knew and their love of the small town of Bitterroot. He'd told her about the latest movie he'd seen and she talked about how many people loved ketchup on their scrambled eggs.

"Earth to Brody," Sawyer said, pulling Brody out of his thoughts.

"Sorry. What did you say?" Brody asked.

"We want you to talk to Cassie about putting up a new shed first thing in the spring," Mac said.

"You know we had plans to replace the old one when we pulled down the storm-damaged one, but discovering those skeletons put everything on hold," Sawyer added. "And as you also know, we need the extra storage space."

"We can't do anything before spring, but I'll mention it to her," Brody replied at the same time his cell phone rang.

He frowned and dug it out of his pocket, surprised

to see Mandy's number. Why would she be calling him this early in the morning? He didn't mind her calling him occasionally, but not during work hours. He excused himself, got up and walked away from the men at the table. He then answered.

"Brody, my father is dead." Her voice exploded over the line, a combination of horror and tears. "He's...he's in his chair and somebody murdered him...they slashed his throat and...and blood... there's so much blood."

Every muscle in his body tensed. "Mandy, have you called Dillon?"

"I... No, not yet." There was a long moment of her weeping.

"Mandy, call Dillon and when he arrives, don't say anything to anyone and don't touch anything. I'll be right there." Brody hung up and hurried over to Sawyer and Mac. "I'm heading out and I don't know when I'll be back."

"What's going on?" Sawyer asked.

"Mandy Wright's father has been murdered." Brody didn't waste time saying another word. He hurried out the door and ran to the shed that held the cowboys' personal vehicles.

The cold air was biting, but not as cold as the thoughts that flew through his head. George Wright murdered? There was no way in hell Brody believed Mandy was responsible for her father's death.

Others would say she had opportunity and some

would believe she had motive. Brody certainly wasn't a lawyer, but she would be the first suspect unless the killer had left a specific calling card.

He knew what it was like to be a suspect. He and all the other men who worked the Holiday Ranch had been suspects first in the seven murders that had taken place so long ago and then more recently when one of their own ranch hands had been murdered. It was easy to appear guilty of a crime even if you had nothing to do with it.

He drove like a bat out of hell, the sound of Mandy's horrified weeping echoing in his head. He never wanted to hear another woman crying with that kind of pain and terror.

Terror... Oh God, was the murderer still in the house with her? Was she in danger right now? Damn, he should have told her to get out of the house.

He slowed long enough to turn in to the long driveway that led to the Wright home. The morning sun shone bright on the white paint of the two-story house.

He recognized both George's and Mandy's cars and realized he had beaten Dillon and his men to the scene of the crime. He parked and hurried out of the truck. He raced to the front door and knocked. It opened and Mandy flew into his arms.

She buried her face in the crook of his neck as deep sobs wrenched through her. He held her tight and stroked her back in an effort to calm her.

"It's going to be okay, Mandy," he murmured.

"No, it's not," she cried. "He's gone and now I'll never have the chance to have a better relationship with him. Nothing is ever going to be okay again." She cried even harder and there was nothing Brody could do to comfort her other than hold her while she wept.

He was still holding her when Chief of Police Dillon Bowie arrived along with two other patrol cars and three of his men. As they parked and then approached the house, Brody finally released Mandy.

"Brody," Dillon greeted him with a touch of surprise in his gray eyes and then turned toward Mandy. "Where is he?"

"In the family room," Mandy replied and began to cry again.

The four men went into the house, and Brody led Mandy through the small living room and into the kitchen. "Sit," he said and gently pushed her down into one of the chairs at the table.

He noticed the nearly full coffeepot on the counter and searched the cabinets until he found two mugs. He poured them each a cup and then sat next to her.

Tears clung to her long lashes as she wrapped her fingers around the coffee mug. "I don't believe this is happening." She gazed up at him, her eyes dark and pain-filled. "Please tell me this is a nightmare and I'm going to wake up and everything will be fine."

"You know I can't tell you that," he replied with a gentleness he hadn't even known he possessed.

She stared down into the mug for several long minutes. The only sounds in the room were the low male voices drifting in from the family room.

"Tell me what you did last night."

Once again she looked up at him, this time with a tiny frown line etched across her brow. "I worked at the café until about six and then went shopping. I got home about eight, wrapped some presents and went to bed."

"Alone?"

He regretted the question the minute it left his lips. A flash of new pain radiated from her eyes. "Yes, alone," she replied curtly.

At that moment Dillon walked into the kitchen. "Mandy, I'm so sorry for your loss. We're waiting now for Teddy to arrive. In the meantime, can I ask you a few questions?" Teddy was Ted Lymon, the medical examiner.

Mandy nodded and Dillon sat in the chair opposite her. "Why would somebody do that to my father? Who would do something like this?" she asked, the words laced with pain.

"That's what I'm going to try to figure out," Dillon replied. "Tell me exactly what happened this morning."

Mandy's pale face and shaking fingers spoke of her despair as she told Dillon about getting up that morning, dressing and then coming into the house to fix her father breakfast.

"Were any of the doors unlocked?" he asked.

"I know the front door wasn't because I used my key to get in, and I can see from here that the back door is still locked," she replied.

"I've got Ben looking at all the windows to check if entry was gained through one of them," Dillon said.

"Do you have an idea of the time of death?" Brody asked.

"Teddy will have to make the official call, but I'd guess sometime in the middle of the night," Dillon replied. "Which brings me to my next question. I know you were shopping yesterday evening, but what did you do after that?"

"I came home and wrapped some presents…" she began.

"And then I came over and spent the night with her." Brody was grateful Mandy didn't look as surprised as he felt as the alibi fell from his lips.

Jeez, what had he just done?

Chapter 4

The next four days went by in a haze for Mandy. She made her father's funeral arrangements and kept in close touch with Dillon about the progress of the investigation. She didn't know how she would have gotten through it all without Brody as a calm and steady presence beside her.

She'd been shocked when he'd told Dillon that he'd been with her on the night of her father's murder. He'd gone even further and told the lawman to check with Fred Ferguson, who would attest to the fact that he and Mandy had also been together on the night of the snowstorm.

She now stood at the front door of the house, waiting for Brody to pick her up for the funeral. It was a beautiful afternoon in the midforties. The sun shone brightly and there wasn't a cloud in the sky.

Grief had also been a big part of the time that had passed since her father's murder. She wasn't sure she grieved for the man himself as much as for the relationship she'd wanted—she'd needed—from him and now would have no opportunity to ever gain.

There were still so many things she had to take care of. She'd been shocked to learn her father had a will on file with an attorney in town and he'd left her everything. In the event of her death her brother would be the beneficiary of what little estate there might be.

Brody had advised her not to make any decisions about things until she'd given herself time to fully grieve, but she'd already decided to clear out the house and put it on the market to sell. She would move to someplace in town, maybe a small house where she could build a life that didn't include the memories of a father who had been so hateful, a man she'd desperately wanted to love her.

She had no idea how many people might attend the funeral this afternoon. She'd been shocked in the last couple of days to realize how many people disliked her father. She knew how he'd treated her, but she hadn't known that he'd carried that same hateful attitude outside the house.

As Brody's truck came up the lane toward the

house, she couldn't help the way her heart beat just a little faster. Although he hadn't touched her in any way since the day she'd discovered her father dead, he'd been the best kind of friend she could ever ask for, and surely that was why her heart quickened at the sight of him.

She turned and hurried to the kitchen to retrieve her purse from the table. By the time she returned to the front door, he was out of his truck and approaching the porch.

Brody Booth in jeans and a flannel shirt was sexy, but Brody in a dark suit coat and slacks was off the charts. She stepped out on the porch, then closed and locked the door behind her.

"Are you ready for this?" he asked as they walked to his truck.

"I guess I'm as ready as I'm going to be. At least I've finally stopped crying all the time."

He opened the passenger door and she slid inside. The truck interior smelled like him…the pleasant scents of sunshine and the outdoors and his woodsy cologne.

"What have you heard from Dillon?" he asked once he was in the truck and had started the engine.

"He called me last night to ask if I knew anything about a pushing and shoving fight my father had last Saturday night at the Watering Hole."

"Who was he pushing and shoving with?"

"Lloyd Green. Apparently Dad owed Lloyd some money and Lloyd tried to collect."

"So, did Dillon say that Lloyd was a suspect in the case?"

"Dillon seems to be playing things close to the vest, but I would assume Lloyd is a suspect." Lloyd worked for Raymond Humes, but that was about all she knew about the older man.

They fell silent and she stared out the window at the barren winter landscape. What would happen after today? When the ceremony was over, would Brody go his own way?

He hadn't exactly signed up for all this. Of course, when he'd offered up the alibi to Dillon, he had to have known that he'd bound them together, at least for a little while.

She was shocked by the new piercing pain that shot through her as she thought of going on without Brody in her life. She'd felt so alone before the night of the snowstorm and his friendship was definitely what was helping her get through these horrible, difficult days.

As he turned in to the Bitterroot Cemetery entrance, she was surprised to see a number of cars parked in the lot. There had been no visitation so this was the one and only opportunity people would have to say a final goodbye to George Wright.

They got out of the truck and were greeted by Dillon and Cassie. "Mandy, I'm so sorry for your loss," Cassie said and took one of Mandy's hands in hers.

The warmth and compassion in her voice made tears spring to Mandy's eyes. "Thank you, Cassie."

"Let me know if there's anything I can do," Cassie added as she released Mandy's hand.

Mandy looked at Dillon. "All anyone can do for me now is to help catch the person who's responsible for my father's murder."

"The investigation is ongoing," he replied.

Julia Hatfield, a waitress at the café, hurried over and pulled Mandy into a tight hug. "Oh, honey, I can't stay long because I have a shift in a little while, but I wanted you to know I'm so sorry, and you come to me if you need anything."

"Thanks, Julia," Mandy replied.

Reverend Wally Johnson walked toward them all, his expression somber and fitting the occasion. "Are we ready to begin?"

Mandy drew in a deep breath and released it, then nodded. It was a bit of a walk to the actual gravesite. Mandy, Brody and Wally led the small crowd over the top of a small rise and then to the place where Mandy's mother rested.

George would be happy resting next to the woman he'd loved. When she'd died she'd taken so much of what little goodness he'd had with her.

They were trailed by several neighbors, a couple

of waitresses from the café, Butch Cooper and two men from the Humes ranch.

Mandy assumed the Humes men might have been her father's drinking buddies. At least Lloyd Green wasn't here. Still, her father probably would have opened the door to Lloyd. Heck, her father would have opened the door to most anyone he knew on the night of his murder. There had been no signs of a break-in or robbery and no hard evidence that anyone had been in the house. The killer must have relocked whatever door he'd entered when he was finished slashing her father's throat.

She glanced up at Brody, so tall and stoic next to her. His very presence helped to calm the tension that had balled up tight in her stomach.

This was it. This was so final. She was now an orphan and she would never, ever be able to get the kind of relationship she'd longed for with her father.

She'd thought she'd cried all the tears in her body, but she'd been wrong. The moment Wally began to speak, tears chased each other down her cheeks.

She would have broken down altogether had Brody not reached out and took her hand in his. The warmth of his hand around hers, the silent support he offered were enough to keep her somewhat in check.

The official ceremony didn't take long. There were no good friends to speak of George in glowing terms and Mandy had declined to speak. When it was over, she told everyone that they were welcome at the house, where sandwiches would be served.

She didn't expect anyone to come. Most of these people who had come had done so to show support for her, which she appreciated.

They were about to leave when Aaron Blair and his wife, Sadie, walked over to the two of them. Aaron was a big man with dark hair, and his wife was a willowy blonde who looked as if she could use a good meal. They owned the ranch next to the Wright place, but Mandy barely knew them.

"Brody... Mandy," Aaron greeted them. "Mandy, I'd tell you I was sorry for your loss, but your father was a mean, spiteful man who nobody will miss."

Mandy took a step backward in stunned shock. "Aaron," his wife replied in surprise.

"Well, it's the truth," Aaron said firmly, raising his square jaw. "George accused me of stealing land from him for years. He accused me of putting up my fencing three feet on his property despite the three surveys I paid for to prove him wrong. He was nothing more than a miserable bastard."

"And I think that's enough," Brody replied in a stern voice. "This isn't the time or the place for you to air your grievances."

"Come on, Aaron. Let's go home," Sadie said. She jerked on her husband's arm and the two of them headed away from the gravesite.

"Don't pay any attention to them," Brody said softly.

Grief once again tightened Mandy's throat. "It doesn't matter if my dad was mean or not. He still didn't deserve to have his throat cut while sitting in his recliner chair in his own home." She swallowed hard against the emotion that rose up in the back of her throat.

"I just hope Dillon is aware of the bad blood between your father and Aaron," Brody replied.

She looked at him in surprise. "Surely you don't think Aaron had anything to do with the murder. I can't imagine it."

"None of us could imagine Adam being a serial killer," he reminded her. He looped his arm through hers. "Come on. Let's get you home."

Together they headed back toward the parking area, but before they got there a man appeared in the distance. Mandy froze at the sight of him.

Was it? Could it be?

She pulled her arm from Brody's, every muscle in her body tensed. "Graham?" The name whispered from her.

As he drew closer and smiled at her, joy exploded in her heart. "Graham!"

She ran toward her brother, half laughing and half crying. She had no idea how he had heard about their father's murder. She didn't care where he had come from. The only thing that mattered was that he was here now.

* * *

Brody didn't like him. He stood in the kitchen with Daisy, who had arrived only moments before with sandwiches, potato salad and baked beans.

Mandy was in the living room, catching up with her brother, and it had taken Brody about two minutes to realize he didn't particularly like and he damned straight didn't trust Graham Wright.

There was no overt reason for his dislike or distrust of the man, other than he'd appeared out of nowhere after being gone for years. It was just a gut instinct that was hard to deny.

About ten people had come back to the house following the funeral, including Dillon and Cassie. They were also in the family room, and Brody hoped Dillon was not only visiting with Graham but also interrogating him as to his whereabouts when George had been murdered.

"Darn, I left the tossed salad out in my car," Daisy said.

"Need some help?" Brody asked.

"Nah, I'll go get it." She left the kitchen by the back door, and at the same time Butch Cooper came in from the family room.

"Hey, Brody," he said and picked up one of the paper plates. "These look good." He grabbed two of the half sandwiches and put them on his plate.

"Daisy doesn't make bad food," he replied. "Even her sandwiches taste better than any I've ever eaten."

Butch nodded and stepped closer to him. "What do you think about the prodigal son's return?"

Brody glanced toward Graham and then looked back at Butch. "The verdict is still out."

Butch nodded. "Yeah, mine, too. Mandy sure is happy to see him."

"I know she's missed him for a very long time." Over the last couple of days Mandy had spoken often about her childhood memories of her brother. She'd believed she would never see him again.

Butch stared down at his plate for a moment and then looked back up. "I'm glad she has you."

There was a softness in the big cowboy's eyes. Brody stared at him. "Does she know you're in love with her?" he asked.

Butch looked as if he might protest and then smiled with a shrug of his shoulders. "It doesn't matter whether she knows it or not. According to her I'm just an ordinary toad and not the prince she's waiting for. It's easy to be crazy about Mandy, but all I want for her is happiness, and right now you seem to be making her happy."

Brody didn't have a chance to tell Butch that it wasn't like that, for at that moment Daisy flew back into the kitchen carrying a large salad bowl. "Here we go," she said.

As Butch continued to fill his plate, Brody moved to the doorway between the kitchen and the family room. The recliner chair where George had been killed had been moved out after Dillon released the house as a crime scene.

Dillon and Cassie sat in straight-backed chairs and Mandy and Graham sat next to each other on the sofa. Graham was telling them about his life in Texas, where he worked as an accountant for a large financial firm.

"I'd stayed in touch with Zeke Osmond over the years, and he called me the minute he heard that my dad was dead," Graham said, a fact that didn't do anything to endear the man to Brody. Zeke worked for Raymond Humes and had long been suspected of being part of the nuisance fires, the stolen cattle and other crimes that had taken place on the Holiday Ranch.

"I can't believe Zeke knew where you were all this time and didn't tell me," Mandy replied.

"I asked him to keep it a secret until I felt like it was time to come back here and see Dad and you in person," Graham replied.

Mandy's eyes sparkled and despite the somber black dress she wore, she looked beautiful. The last few days had been more difficult for him than he'd ever expected.

While Mandy had grieved, he had lusted. The scent of her stirred him like no other, and no matter what she wore he found her sexy as hell. This wasn't the way a friendship was supposed to work.

The minute he'd provided her an alibi to Dillon,

Brody had known that he'd thrown himself into a relationship with her, at least until her father's murder was solved.

Maybe now that Graham was back in her life Mandy wouldn't care if Brody distanced himself from her. Maybe she'd stop calling him late in the evenings just to say good-night. This might be his opportunity to step away from her.

And he needed to step away from her. He'd started looking forward to her good-night calls. He dreamed of capturing her lips with his, of stroking her naked curves and more. He didn't want or need anyone in his life, especially a woman who was looking for her prince. He was definitely no prince.

"Where were you on the night your father was murdered?" Dillon leaned forward in his chair.

Graham smiled. He had a smile just like Mandy's... wide and warm. "I was at a company Christmas party. I'll be happy to give you names of people who were there with me and will corroborate that I attended."

"And after the party ended?" Dillon's expression was pleasant enough but his gray eyes were hard and cold. Those same cold eyes had been directed at Brody when Dillon believed one of the Holiday Ranch cowboys was guilty of murder.

"The party didn't break up until after one or so and then I went to my fiancée's apartment and spent the night there," Graham replied.

"I can't believe you'd think he's guilty of anything," Mandy said to Dillon with a touch of outrage.

"Honey, now isn't the time or the place," Cassie said softly to Dillon.

"Of course," Dillon replied and sat back in his chair. "But I would like to speak to you later," he added to Graham.

"I'll be glad to," Graham replied.

Butch and some of the others left and eventually everyone else got up, filled a plate and found places to sit at the table. The talk turned to what Mandy intended to do with the property.

"I need to clean out everything. I'll donate Dad's clothes and the furniture, and then I'm going to sell." She looked at her brother seated next to her. "I'll split everything fifty-fifty with you, Graham."

"I don't need your money, Mandy," he replied. "I've done pretty well for myself. Besides, that's not why I came back here."

"Why did you come back?" The words blurted out of Brody.

Graham frowned. "I came back because not a day went by that I didn't think about my little sister." He gazed at Mandy. "I was always sorry that I left you behind, but we were both so young." He looked at Brody. "When I heard about the murder, I knew I needed to see Mandy and make sure she was okay."

Mandy reached across the table and grabbed one

of his hands. "It doesn't matter. Nothing matters other than you're here now."

"I'm here until just after the first of the year, and then I need to get back to my job and my life in Dallas," he replied.

"And I can't wait to hear all about your life in Dallas," Mandy replied.

Brody glanced at his watch. The day was fading away and he needed to leave. He had someplace he had to be in thirty minutes.

"Mandy, I need to head out," he said.

She jumped up from the table. "Okay, I'll walk you out."

She grabbed her coat from the hall tree and shrugged it on. Together they walked out into the fading light of day. "Brody, I can't thank you enough for everything you've done to support me over the last couple of days."

"It was my pleasure," he replied.

"I really don't know what I would have done without you." They reached his truck's driver's door and she gazed up at him with her gorgeous dark-lashed eyes. "You aren't going to stop being my friend just because I have a brother now, are you?"

Although that was exactly what he'd intended to do, there was no way he could look into her soulful eyes and tell her that…especially not today of all days. "Of course not," he replied.

She grinned, suddenly threw her arms around his

neck and pressed her lips firmly against his cheek. His body immediately responded to her body so close to his and to the warmth of her lips against his skin.

"What's that for?" he asked gruffly as she released her hold on him.

"That's for being the best friend I could ever ask for," she replied. "I'll call you later?"

"Sounds good," he said.

He watched while she hurried back into the house. Adrenaline still whipped through him. He needed to lift a car or cut down a tree or do something physical to rid himself of the unwanted surge of desire inside him.

He got into his truck and pulled away from the Wright place, grateful that he was on his way to spend some time with Ellie.

Chapter 5

Mandy released a sigh that blew a strand of hair away from her face. She placed a box of books next to the doorway in her father's bedroom and then looked up at her brother, who was emptying dresser drawers.

"I think we need to take a break," she said. They had been working nonstop for the past two hours, ever since Mandy had gotten off work at the café.

Graham stopped working and sank down on the edge of the bed. "The last time I was in this room it was Mother's sewing room," he said.

"Dad moved down here about a month after you left. I think he couldn't stand being in the master bedroom upstairs without Mom."

She scanned the small room. "At least we've made some progress tonight."

"Actually, I'm going to take off in just a few minutes. It's getting late and I'm supposed to meet Zack and a couple of other guys at the Watering Hole for drinks in about fifteen minutes."

"Why didn't you tell me you had plans? I wouldn't have asked you to come over here tonight."

He smiled at her, the gentle smile she remembered from her childhood. "I know you want to get the house packed up and off your back as soon as possible. I can definitely help out all day tomorrow."

"You don't have to lift a finger to help me. I'm just glad you're here and we got some time to visit more," she replied. "Besides, for the next couple of days I'm working at the café."

"What are your plans for the rest of the evening? Is Brody coming over?"

"No, I'm going to work here for another hour or two and then head back to my apartment." It was funny how just the sound of Brody's name could stir something deep inside her.

It was also funny that even after spending the day before catching up with Graham, there was still so much for the two of them to share about their missing years.

Together the two siblings left the bedroom and walked toward the front door. Graham pulled on his coat and then turned to face her. "Don't work too hard tonight. We have a couple of weeks to get everything done."

"I know. But I did call Seth Richardson, who runs the youth program here in town, and told him he could come by in a couple of days and pick up some of the furniture. The youth center could always use another sofa and some chairs."

"That's good of you," he replied.

"The youth center is one of my passions, along with cooking," she said. She'd always believed that if the youth center had been in existence when she and Graham were growing up, then maybe Graham wouldn't have run away.

"So, what is the plan for tomorrow?"

"I'm pretty booked up working at the café, and I told Seth I'd be in the kissing booth as usual tomorrow night. I should probably ask Daisy for some days off so you and I can have more time together."

"No, I don't want you changing your schedule just because I'm in town. I'll work around your schedule. I'm still catching up with old friends, too."

"I'm working for three days and then I'm off for several. Maybe then we can spend some time together and get the rest of the things packed up here."

Once again he smiled at her. "Just remember, Mandy, I'm back in your life for the rest of our lives. Call me when you're ready to tackle some more of this mess, and in the meantime I'll probably see you in the café." He stepped out into the cold, dark evening. "I'll talk to you tomorrow."

Mandy watched until the taillights of his rental car disappeared from her view, and then she closed the door and returned to the family room.

She flopped down on the sofa and once again expelled a deep sigh. She was exhausted, but there was so much to do. She hadn't realized how much of a pack rat her father had been. She certainly hadn't expected Graham to help her, but it was great that he'd offered, and he continued to catch her up on what she considered his lost years when they hadn't been in contact.

She leaned back, and instead of thinking about the work that still had to be done, her thoughts remained on her brother. She'd told him he could stay here in the house while he was in Bitterroot, but he'd insisted he was fine at the motel.

Last night after the funeral, they had visited with each other until well after midnight. He'd told her about hitching a ride with a truck driver to Dallas, and about the foster family who had taken him in after the police had picked him up on the streets.

According to him they had been a strict but loving family who had helped him through college and continued to be a part of his life.

He'd talked about his fiancée, Nancy, who he obviously loved to distraction. She was also an accountant where Graham worked, and according to him she was one of the sweetest, most kind people on the face of the earth. Mandy couldn't wait to meet her.

She'd shared with him a lot of things about her own life, but she hadn't told Graham about her father's verbal and mental abuse. There was no reason for him to know about that now.

She still didn't know everything about the relationship her father and her brother had shared before Graham had chosen to run away. None of that mattered now. All that was important was the promise of having her brother back in her life for good.

She pulled herself up off the sofa. She still wanted to pack a couple more boxes of books in her father's bedroom before calling it a night. Tomorrow or the next day she would drop the books off at the local library, which always appreciated donations.

As she worked, her thoughts went to Brody, which they had far too often since the night of the snowstorm. He'd been so wonderful through her shock at her father's murder and then when she'd had to make the arrangements for the funeral.

However, when she'd kissed him on the cheek, a river of unexpected desire had flowed through her. It had been sharp and aching, and she'd wanted desperately to press her lips against his.

But she'd suspected that if she acted inappropriately as a friend, he'd run for the hills. He'd been quite firm when he'd told her he wasn't looking for a woman in his life, and nothing he had done or said since the night of the snowstorm had made her believe he'd changed his mind.

Suddenly oddly depressed, she went back to the bedroom, finished packing a box and then decided to quit for the night. She was just about to leave the room when she heard the whoosh that indicated the front door had opened.

"Graham?" she called out. Maybe he'd forgotten something. There was no reply.

"Graham, is that you?" She stepped out of the bedroom and into the hall. A horrified gasp escaped her as she saw a man at the other end of the hallway wearing a ski mask and holding a knife.

For a brief moment her mind refused to work, and then questions slammed into it. Who was he? What did he want? Why was he in the house?

It was only when he took his first menacing step toward her that she unfroze and raced back into her father's bedroom. Her heart thundered so loud in her head she couldn't hear anything else. She refused to take any more time to think about who the person was or why he was in her house. He had a ski mask and a knife...that was all she needed to know.

With no lock on the bedroom door and no time to do anything else, she slammed the door and then sat with her back against it. She frantically fumbled in her sweatshirt pocket for her cell phone.

She punched in Dillon's number, but before he could answer the doorknob turned and the door pressed inward. She screamed, and she was still screaming when Dillon answered. "Hurry, Dillon, there's an intruder in the house and he's after me."

She barely got the words out before she was forcefully moved forward about an inch along the floor and the door opened just a crack.

Screaming again, she dropped her cell phone and shoved with all her might against the door. It slammed shut once again, and this time she reached up over her head and grabbed the doorknob in an effort to keep it from turning.

"I called the police," she yelled. "They will be here any minute."

Another scream released from her as the doorknob jiggled beneath her grasp. She held tight as frightened tears blurred her vision.

What was happening? Who was this person? What was he going to do if he managed to get in? "You'd better leave now if you don't want to be arrested," she cried desperately.

The jiggling stopped.

Several long minutes passed and there was nothing, no sound, no jiggling and no pressure against the door. But the lack of those things didn't make her terror abate at all. She squeezed her eyes closed and held tight to the doorknob.

Was he standing on the other side of the door, just waiting for her to let down her guard, to release her death grip on the doorknob? Or had he left the house and was now making his way to one of the two windows in the bedroom in an effort to get to her?

Panic hitched her breath as her gaze shot to first one window and then the other. So far all she could see was the darkness of night in the cracks between the navy curtains that hung there.

Her hands ached with her efforts to hold so tight to the knob. Frightened tears continued to fall, and she held on for dear life.

She nearly wept with relief when she heard the sounds of sirens in the distance. Help was on the way and she just needed to hang on for a few more minutes. The sirens drew closer and then stopped.

A moment of silence, running footsteps and then… "Mandy?" Dillon's familiar voice drifted through the bedroom door.

She got to her feet, grabbed her cell phone and opened the door. As she realized she was safe, a renewed terror gripped her by the throat. Dear God, somebody had come after her with a knife.

"Call Brody," she said to Dillon as her body began to shake uncontrollably and an icy chill filled her.

"Let's get you into the family room," Dillon said gently.

She nodded and followed him out of the hallway. Her trembling legs carried her just as far as the edge of the sofa, where she collapsed.

She looked at the two officers who had accompanied Dillon. "Please, would somebody please call Brody and ask him to come over."

She desperately needed Brody beside her. She wanted him to wrap her in his big, strong arms and warm her, reassure her that she was really safe.

"I'll call him," Officer Juan Ramirez said and disappeared into the kitchen.

Dillon sat on the opposite end of the sofa and pulled out a small notepad and pen. "Now, tell me exactly what happened."

"Graham and I spent a couple of hours boxing things up. When he left to meet some buddies for drinks, I decided to work for a little while longer by myself." She shivered and wrapped her arms around herself. "I was back in the bedroom and heard the front door open. I stepped out into the hallway, and a man was standing there wearing a ski mask and holding a knife."

She paused for a moment, the terror of that moment screaming inside her once again. She swallowed once...twice and then continued. "He started toward me, and I ran back in the bedroom and closed the door. I managed to call you, and then I held on tight to the doorknob and sat in front of the door so he couldn't get in."

There was no doubt in her mind that if Dillon hadn't arrived when he had, eventually the man would have gotten through the door. And God knew what would have happened to her then.

"Was the front door locked?" Dillon asked.

She frowned thoughtfully. Had she locked it after Graham had left or had she just closed the door? "I don't remember," she answered with frustration. "Maybe not." How could she be so stupid in not consciously locking the door? Her father had been murdered in this house.

"Did you recognize anything about the man?" Dillon asked.

She shook her head. "Since he wore the ski mask, I don't even know what color hair he had."

"What about his body type? What was he wearing?"

She frowned. "Maybe a little bit tall and a medium build? I... I don't know what he was wearing. Everything happened so fast. I saw the knife, ran back in the bedroom and slammed the door."

"Are you sure it was a man?"

Mandy stared at him. "I can't be absolutely sure, but I thought it was a man."

"It's too bad all the snow has melted away. Otherwise we might have been able to get some good footprints," Dillon replied, his own frustration evident in his tone.

A vision of the slash across her father's throat filled her head. Somebody had done that with a knife. Had it been the same man? If so, then why had he come after her? What had she done to warrant such an attack?

"Excuse me for a minute." Dillon got up and motioned for Officer Ben Taylor to follow him into the kitchen.

One she was left alone, the memory of finding her father dead again filled her mind. The scent of death filled her nose and a faint nausea rose up in the back of her throat.

A simmering hysteria pressed tight against her chest as she thought of those moments when she'd been sure the man was going to get inside the bedroom. And if he had...

The sound of the front door opening shot a fight-or-flight response through her. She bolted up from the sofa, every muscle tensed.

"Mandy?" Brody stepped into the room.

"Brody." With a sob, she launched herself into his arms.

Brody held Mandy as she cried and haltingly told him through her tears what had happened. He was still holding her when Dillon and two of his men entered the room from the kitchen.

Ben Taylor nodded to him and then went out the front door. Dillon and Juan waited patiently until Mandy had pulled herself together enough to sit back down on the sofa.

She held Brody's hand in a death grip, and a simmering anger filled Brody's chest. Who had come after her and why? The idea of any harm coming to her spiked his anger into a near rage.

"It's possible the intruder came in to rob the place," Dillon said.

"With a knife?" Brody replied with obvious disbelief.

"Maybe he pulled the knife when he heard Mandy."

"If it was a robbery attempt then why didn't he just leave when he heard her voice? Why come after her at all?" Brody asked.

Dillon released a sigh. "Maybe he came after her because she saw him."

"But she said she called out. He must have heard her. Why didn't he run then?" Brody pressed.

"I don't have the answers yet, but I'll get them," Dillon replied.

"I hope you're checking on where Graham was at the time of the intrusion," Brody said.

"Graham? He wouldn't try to kill me," Mandy protested.

"I've already dispatched Ben to check on Graham's whereabouts," Dillon replied.

"What about Aaron Blair?" Mandy asked. "He hated my father, and maybe his hatred has bled over to me."

Dillon frowned. "What makes you think Aaron hated your father?"

Brody looked at her in surprise. "You didn't tell

him about what Aaron said on the day of the funeral?"

Her cheeks dusted with a faint color. "With Graham showing up, I forgot." She told Dillon about the bad blood between her father and his neighbor.

"Mandy, I hate to tell you, but there was plenty of bad blood between your father and several men in town," Dillon said.

"Are these men suspects in George's murder?" Brody asked. Dillon gave a curt nod of his head. "Then tell me who they are." Brody wanted the names of the men who might be a danger to the woman holding his hand tightly as if it were a lifeline in a storm-tossed sea.

Dillon sank down in the chair opposite them. "I'm assuming you know that your father owed Lloyd Green some money, but that's not the only person in town he owed. He also apparently borrowed some money from Jimbo King."

Mandy's eyes widened. "Jimbo King? Why on earth would Dad borrow anything from that man?"

"That man" not only ran a sleazy cash loaning operation but also owned a pawn business/motorcycle shop that catered to a rough clientele.

"I don't know, but what I do know is that your father walked out of Jimbo's business with a car title loan and two thousand dollars cash," Dillon said. "That's why I think the intruder tonight might have been looking for that cash."

"I certainly haven't found any money around here," Mandy said. "I have no idea what he might have done with the cash. I've seen his bank records and he didn't deposit it."

"And then there's Nate Cameron," Dillon continued. "Apparently he and your father have had a beef with each other for years. They almost came to blows in the convenience store a week before your father's murder."

Mandy held up her hand as if she'd heard enough. "Okay, my father had enemies, but that still doesn't answer why that man came after me tonight."

"I know," Dillon replied, his eyes dark and filled with aggravation. "Look, we've only been investigating your father's murder for less than a week. As to what happened here tonight, I don't have any answers. All I can tell you is that from now on, if you're working here you need to make sure you have somebody with you."

"Don't worry. I'll see that she's safe," Brody replied. He believed Dillon wasn't taking this threat seriously enough, that the lawman truly believed it had been a robbery attempt gone bad.

Brody didn't know what to believe. He only knew that Mandy had nobody to depend on except a brother who had been gone from her life for years.

She'd told him she needed a friend and he'd stepped into that role. Now she needed him to protect her from whatever the hell was going on.

She didn't have any real girlfriends, and the idea of her being all alone in her apartment over the garage on this isolated property was untenable, especially given what had just happened tonight.

Dillon asked a few more questions as Juan worked on the bedroom door to see if he could lift any prints until Mandy remembered the man had worn gloves.

"Why can I now remember him wearing gloves and can't remember anything else about him?" she asked in frustration.

"You might remember something else later," Dillon replied. "And if you do, call me."

"And you'll call me later and tell me about the alibis of some of the men you've mentioned?" Brody asked.

"Yes, please call Brody," Mandy said and rubbed a hand across the center of her forehead. "Are we done here? All I want to do now is get back to my own place."

"Yeah, I think we're done here," Dillon replied. He looked at Brody. "I'll call you with an update later this evening."

Brody nodded, but he doubted any answers would be forthcoming so soon. Once the lawmen were gone, Brody stood from the sofa. "Take a ride with me?" he asked.

She also got up from the sofa and eyed him curiously. "Okay, but where?"

"Back to the Holiday Ranch so I can pack a bag. I'm moving in with you, Mandy."

Her eyes widened and her lower lip trembled slightly. "You don't believe it was a robbery gone bad?"

He hesitated a moment and then replied, "I don't know exactly what to believe. All I know is that right now, with everything that has happened, I'm not comfortable with you staying out here all alone."

He didn't even want to think about how difficult staying with her might be on him. But he didn't want anything happening to her, and the night's events had scared him for her.

"Maybe it would be nice to have you around for a day or two," she replied. "Hopefully by then Dillon will have some answers for us."

They pulled on their coats, and minutes later they were in his truck and headed to the Holiday Ranch. "I'm being very selfish in wanting you with me," she said. "Maybe I could just talk to Graham and have him stay with me."

"Would you be comfortable with that?"

She released a small sigh. "Not really. I mean, he's my brother and I love him and I'm happy he's back, but we still don't know each other very well."

Brody was glad she didn't want Graham moving in. Right now he didn't trust anyone with her safety except himself and the lawmen of Bitterroot.

"Brody, what about your own work? The last thing

I want to do is make things difficult for you," she said with obvious concern.

"Don't you worry about me. The other men will cover for me until we figure things out."

"At least for the next couple of days I'm working full shifts at the café, and then I'm supposed to work the kissing booth for a couple of hours each evening."

"Then starting tomorrow I'll take you to work in the morning and pick you up when your shift is over, and I'll just hang out while you're working the kissing booth." His hands tightened around the steering wheel. He was surprised to realize he didn't really like the idea of her kissing other cowboys even if it was for charity.

At least he knew she'd be safe while working at the café. Nobody would dare attempt to harm her with so many people around her as witnesses.

"Brody, I'm just a little bit scared." Her soft voice held a faint appeal and he sensed she was looking for some reassurance from him.

He had no assurance to give her. "Mandy, I want you to be a little scared. Right now we don't know the motive or the identity of the person who came after you. I want you to be wary of every male in this town."

"Gee, thanks for making me feel better," she replied drily.

He flashed her a forced smile. "That's what friends are for."

They reached the ranch and Brody parked his truck in front of the cowboy motel, a long building of small rooms where the cowboys lived. They got out of the truck and she followed him into his small room.

"So, this is where you live," she said as she looked around.

Brody pulled a duffel bag from beneath the single bed. "I've lived here since I was fourteen," he replied.

She frowned. "You don't have much to show you've been here for that long."

She was talking about the bare walls. There was nothing personal to indicate the room was his. He had no family photos, and no landscape painting that he'd ever seen spoke to him enough to buy and hang it.

He didn't collect fishing or hunting gear or beer steins. He just existed in this room when he wasn't at work or in the cowboy dining room with the other men.

It took him only minutes to pack enough items for the night. He could grab some more things tomorrow while she was working at the café.

"Thank you for what you're doing for me, Brody," she said when they were almost back at her place.

"I'll admit we may be overreacting to what happened tonight. Maybe it really was somebody who read about your dad's death and assumed nobody would be in the house. Maybe the rumor got out that your dad had a lot of cash stashed someplace, but I'm just not willing to take that chance right now." He glanced over at her and caught her smiling at him, a beautiful smile lighted by the dashboard illumination and one that shot a streak of heat into his stomach.

"I have to warn you, the apartment is kind of small," she said as they got out of the truck in front of the detached garage.

"You saw where I stay," he replied. "We'll manage just fine for a night or two."

It was just after ten o'clock as he followed her up the stairs to the living quarters. She unlocked the door, and he stepped into an explosion of color and scent that instantly increased the heat that whirled around inside him.

It smelled of Mandy, that intoxicating scent of vanilla and sugar and warm, inviting woman. There was a black sofa with pink throw pillows, and the bed against one of the walls wore a black-and-pink polka-dot bedspread. The space was definitely feminine and he was instantly a bit ill at ease.

"Make yourself at home," she said and shrugged out of her coat. He took off his and sank down on the sofa. Thank God there was a sofa, because he didn't know if he could stand a night of sleeping in bed with her as a "friend."

"Would you like anything to eat or drink?" she asked.

"No thanks. I think the best thing we both can do is get a good night's sleep." He pointed to the door they'd entered. "Is that the only way in?"

"Yes."

Brody took his gun out of his holster and set it on the coffee table. "Then it will be easy to make sure nobody gets inside. Do you mind giving me a pillow and a blanket? I'll just bunk here on the sofa." He sat once again.

"You know you don't have to sleep on the sofa." She gestured toward the bed. "It's a queen size, and it isn't as if we haven't slept in the same bed before."

"Yes, but I've never thought you might be in danger before. I intend to sleep with one eye open, and that makes me restless. It's better if I'm on the sofa," he replied. He hoped like hell that sounded like a reasonable excuse.

"Okay. Would you like to use the bathroom first to get ready for bed or do you want me to?"

"You go ahead," he replied. He could use a few minutes to acclimate himself to this new space and to attempt to get the damnable heat of hungry desire for her out of his body.

She grabbed some clothing from a drawer and then disappeared into what he assumed was the bathroom. The sound of the shower running pulled him up off the sofa again. In the kitchenette area there were two windows. He checked to make sure both of them were locked and then walked over to the window next to the bed and checked it as well.

He double-checked the door to make sure it was locked up tight and then paused to look at several pictures that hung on the wall. The first one was a photo of Graham and Mandy with Graham's arm slung around his younger sister and big smiles on their faces. Brody would guess Mandy to be about six and Graham about ten.

The next photo was of George and his daughter and what looked like her high school graduation day. Mandy wore the traditional cap and gown and a strained smile. George looked like he'd rather have been anywhere but in the picture.

The ring of Brody's cell phone pulled him away from the photos. It was Dillon. "I just thought you'd want to know that Graham was at the Watering Hole when Mandy was attacked. Half a dozen people corroborated his presence there, and they were all locals who would have no reason to lie for him."

"Thanks, Dillon. Anyone else look likely as the attacker?"

"I've got nothing else right now to report. And just to give you a heads-up, I think Graham is on his way over there to check on Mandy." They ended the call. So, Graham hadn't been the person who attacked Mandy. That was definitely good to know.

Within minutes a knock fell on the door. Brody assumed it was Graham, but just to be safe he picked up his gun from the coffee table and carried it with him to the door.

"Brody, is she all right?" Graham asked worriedly as Brody allowed him inside.

"Physically she's fine. Mentally she's a bit shaken up."

"Thank God you're here with her, and obviously on protection duty," Graham replied with a nod at Brody's gun.

Before either of them could say anything more, Mandy came out of the bathroom. She was clad in a pair of red flannel pajamas with little snowmen. Her hair was damp and her cheeks were flushed.

How in the hell could a woman in flannel look so damned sexy?

Graham walked over and pulled his sister into a quick hug. Then the three of them sat at the small kitchen table. "Mandy, I'm so sorry. If I'd have known somebody was going to break into the house I would have never left you alone there."

Brody had to admit, the man looked genuinely upset. "So when you left, I guess you didn't see anyone lurking around or a car parked close to the house?" he asked.

Graham shook his head. "I told Dillon I didn't see anyone or anything to make me believe something was amiss. Believe me, I wish I would have seen somebody." He turned his gaze to Mandy. "Sis, from now on we work together in the house and you aren't ever left alone there."

"I'll make sure she isn't left alone anywhere," Brody replied. "I'm staying here with her for a few days."

"That's a relief," Graham replied with a nod. "And now, I know it's late. I just needed to assure myself that you were really okay."

"I'm okay," Mandy replied. "All's well that ends well, right?" She smiled at both of the men.

"Then I'll just get out of here," Graham replied. They all got up from their chairs. Once again he hugged Mandy. "I'm so glad that man didn't get to you. I can't imagine why anyone would want to hurt you."

"That makes two of us. I have to admit I've never been so frightened in my whole life, but I'm going to be fine now," she said.

Moments later Graham was gone and Brody was in the bathroom, taking a quick shower. Had it been George's murderer who had come into the house to chase Mandy with a knife? Had that been the same knife that had so brutally slashed her father's throat?

Despite the warmth of the shower, a chill tried to work its way through him. He couldn't imagine why anyone would want to harm Mandy.

Maybe it had been somebody who had heard that George had received a large sum of cash from Jimbo, and that same somebody had believed it was stashed someplace in the house. Perhaps Dillon had been right after all.

But that scenario just didn't ring true, not considering the man's actions when he'd heard Mandy's voice. Why hadn't he just turned tail and run back into the night? The house had been empty during most of the days since the funeral. Why not break in then to search for any money?

By the time he got out of the shower and dressed in a clean white T-shirt and a pair of jeans, equally troubling thoughts drifted through his head.

In all the years he'd lived in Bitterroot, he'd never gotten involved in other people's problems. He'd worked his job and defended the ranch against anyone who tried to do harm, but other than that he'd been a solitary man who shared very little of himself with anyone.

What was it about Mandy Wright that had him doing so many things out of character? It was as if she expected him to be a better man than he was and somehow he was trying to live up to those unrealistic expectations.

Most people gave him a wide berth, but not Mandy. He shoved these thoughts away. She was nothing more to him that a woman in trouble and he just happened to be in a position to help her. It was nothing more than that and nothing less.

He left the bathroom and blinked in surprise. All the lights were off except a lamp next to Mandy's bed and the glow of two lit candles on the same nightstand. The room now smelled of apples and cinnamon with an underlying fragrance he'd come to know as hers.

"I hope you don't mind the candles. I always light a couple before I go to sleep."

"I don't mind," he replied. The candles were short in the tall jar containers and hell yes, he minded the candles that painted her face in beautiful shadows and light. Hell yes, he minded the candles that made the room feel so much smaller and more intimate.

He walked over to the sofa and found a bed pillow and a soft hot-pink blanket. Thank God none of the other cowboys would know he was sleeping under a pink blanket. He'd never hear the end of it. He placed his gun on the coffee table, unfolded the blanket and then stretched out.

"All settled?" she asked.

"I'm good," he replied.

She turned off the lamp, leaving only the candlelight radiance to create a small illumination. Too much illumination. From his vantage point he could see her snuggled beneath the covers. He closed his eyes.

"Brody?"

"Yeah?" He answered without opening his eyes.

"Somehow, someway I'll make this all up to you."

Visions instantly exploded in his head, erotic visions of the two of them making love. He jerked his head to halt them. "You don't have to make anything up to me," he said gruffly. "Now, let's get some sleep."

"Okay. Good night, Brody."

"Good night," he replied.

Seconds ticked by and then minutes. When he finally opened his eyes once again she appeared to be sleeping. Candlelight danced across her features, highlighting her brows, her cheekbones and her full lips.

He couldn't be her friend. She was too much of a temptation and he couldn't be friends with a woman he wanted. He didn't want to be friends with anyone.

He'd see her through this threat, and then he had to walk away from her and never look back.

Chapter 6

"You look chipper for a woman who was attacked last night," Daisy said to Mandy when she entered the café the next morning. "Does that have anything to do with the cowboy who just dropped you off?" She raised one of her bright red penciled eyebrows.

"No, it's nothing like that." Mandy felt her cheeks warm with color despite the protest. "Brody is just being a really good friend right now."

"Sounds like you need one. So, tell me exactly what happened last night," Daisy replied. "Zeke Osmond was in earlier and said that you'd been attacked in your father's house."

By the time Mandy finished telling Daisy about

the events that had happened the night before, the morning rush had begun. Mandy hurried into the back room, grabbed an apron and tied it around her waist, then raced back to the dining room to begin her work for the day.

She smiled and poured coffee and took and delivered orders, and all the while her thoughts were consumed with Brody. It had been so reassuring last night to fall asleep and know he was mere footsteps away from her. The only thing better would have been to have him in her bed.

The idea of being held in his arms, of his sensual lips kissing hers filled her with a desire she'd never known before. What was it about him that stirred her so deeply?

It wasn't just a sexual thing. She wanted to know everything about him…what he thought and what he dreamed about and why he had chosen to go through life alone. She had a feeling he had secrets, and she wished he'd share them with her.

Thoughts of Brody fled her mind as she approached the booth where three young women sat. Dana Witherspoon, Vanessa Hightower and Miranda Silver had all gone to high school with Mandy.

They had all been cheerleaders, the golden girls everyone wanted to be. They had been some of the girls who had whispered and snickered about Mandy behind her back, although in recent years two of them had mellowed out. Dana still remained more than a bit of a smug twit.

"Good morning, ladies," Mandy said briskly as she pulled out her order pad.

Miranda smiled, although the gesture didn't quite reach her eyes. Mandy had heard she'd just gone through a painful divorce. Mandy also knew Miranda and her husband had two children. "Good morning, Mandy," she replied.

"We all want to start out with coffee," Dana said imperiously. "And please make sure it's fresh."

"Coming right up," Mandy replied and hurried to retrieve one of the full coffeepots from the warmers.

"We heard about what happened to you last night," Vanessa said when Mandy returned with the coffee. "I'm so glad you're okay."

"Of course we're glad you're all right. Otherwise who would be pouring our coffee this morning?" Dana said and then tittered as if it were an amusing joke. Miranda stared down at her menu and Vanessa stared at the wall someplace over Mandy's shoulder. The awkward moment passed as Mandy took their food orders.

She'd just finished serving the three women their meals when Jimbo King and two of his lackeys walked in and took a table in her section.

There was no way Jimbo had been the man at her father's home the night before. The big bald man had to weigh at least three hundred pounds. However, either of the two men with him could have been the person who had raised the knife and chased her into the bedroom.

Should she mention the money her father owed him? Her father's bank account had a whopping hundred and twenty dollars in it at the time of his death. Mandy certainly didn't have the money to pay the big man back, and in any case it wasn't her debt to pay. Still, she was honorable enough to see to it that he got his money when the ranch sold and the estate was fully settled.

"Morning, gentlemen. What can I start you off with today?" she asked with a forced brightness to her tone.

"Coffee and a glass of orange juice for me," Jimbo said.

"That sounds good to me," Sean Watters replied as he shoved a strand of his greasy brown hair off his forehead.

"Me, too," Donny Pruitt added.

Mandy scurried away to get their drinks, grateful the subject of the money her father owed hadn't come up. It didn't come up until she'd served their meals and had returned to refill their coffee. As she reached for Jimbo's cup, his big, meaty hand snaked around her wrist.

"We need to talk, girly."

She tried to pull away, but he held tight. "Jimbo, I know my father borrowed money from you and

I'll see you get it back, but it's going to take some time," she said.

He let go of her. "Time is money and interest is accruing."

"Can't you forget about interest? I mean, Dad is dead."

"Business is business. I want my money."

"Try to remember that I'm not the one who owes that money and I have no real responsibility to pay it back." Although her heart fluttered wildly in her chest, she faced him boldly. "Maybe somebody on your payroll tried to get that cash back last night by breaking into the house?"

Jimbo's dark gaze held hers, unreadable and slightly menacing. "Breaking into the house? I don't know what you're talking about. Now, how about that coffee?"

She didn't breathe easily again until Jimbo and his two thugs had left the building. By then it was time for her break, and she carried a cup of coffee into the back room and sank down on one of the chairs at the four-top table.

"Are you okay?" Daisy walked into the room and sank down in a chair opposite Mandy.

"I'm fine. Why?"

"I noticed you got a little quiet on the floor."

Mandy looked at her boss in surprise. "I didn't think it showed." She took a sip of her coffee and then sighed. "It feels like my dad died owing money to everyone in town, including Jimbo."

Daisy's eyes opened wider. "Did Jimbo give you a hard time when he was here?"

Mandy rubbed her wrist where he had grabbed it. "He just reminded me that a debt was owed."

"That man is a complete disgrace to this town," Daisy said scornfully. "He takes advantage of people in trouble with that cash and pawn shop he runs."

"I just can't imagine why Dad got money from him and what happened to that money."

Daisy narrowed her eyes. "Do you think one of those weasels he had with him broke into your dad's place last night?"

Mandy thought of Sean and Donny and then shrugged her shoulders. "It could have been one of them, or it could have been somebody else. I just wish I had some answers instead of so many questions."

"Are you being careful?"

She nodded. "That's why I have Brody being my unofficial bodyguard right now. Thank goodness he wanted to help keep me safe."

"He's a good one. He keeps most people away just by that dark look on his face."

Mandy leaned forward. "Oh, Daisy, but you should see him when he smiles," she replied. "It's like a pure ray of sunshine after a cold, cloudy day."

Daisy sat back in the chair and grinned at her.

"Now, that sure doesn't sound like just friends to me. You sound like a woman who's gone all weak-kneed over a man."

"Oh no," Mandy replied hurriedly. "I'm just saying he has a very nice smile."

"I wouldn't know. I don't believe I've ever seen it. And it won't be long before the lunch crowd starts to arrive, so I'll just get out of here and let you have the rest of your break in peace." Daisy got up from the table and left.

Mandy curled her fingers around her coffee cup and replayed Daisy's words in her mind. Was she going all weak in the knees for Brody? Even if she was, it wouldn't matter. She could go completely weak-kneed and fall on the floor but that didn't mean he'd pick her up and proclaim his love for her.

And why was she sitting here thinking about love with anyone?

She had a house to clear out, her father's debts to pay, a brother to continue to get to know and the potential of her father's killer for some reason wanting her dead, as well. The last thing she needed on her mind was love.

She had a feeling there was no way Brody Booth could be the prince she'd been waiting for. Her prince would want to bond with her mentally and physically. Brody was reticent to share his feelings and thoughts and definitely didn't seem to desire her.

A friend. That was all she needed right now.

Somebody she could trust and depend on, a person she could confide in. She needed somebody who would shelter her from harm until they figured out what was going on.

Somebody like Brody.

She shoved thoughts of him aside as she finished her break and headed back out to take care of the lunch customers.

Brody sat tall in the saddle as he roamed through the herd of cattle, looking for any that might be sick or hurt. It was a daily chore on the Holiday Ranch. Coyote attacks or illness could devastate the assets that kept the ranch financially sound.

It was another cold day, although the sun was bright overhead. Thankfully there was no more snow forecast for the next few days.

Personally, he had no idea what to expect over the next couple of days. All he knew was staying with Mandy was going to test his self-control.

He had awakened that morning before her and had crept into the bathroom to wash up for the day. When he'd left the bathroom she'd been up and scampering around in those snowman pajamas, the bright red color doing amazing things to her skin tone and dark hair.

She'd made coffee and had offered to make him breakfast. He'd declined the offer, just wanting her to get dressed in real clothes. He'd finally breathed a sigh of relief when she'd taken her clothing for the day and disappeared into the bathroom. Thank God she was manning the booth tonight so they wouldn't be in the small quarters of her apartment for too long before going to sleep.

He glanced at his watch. It was time for him to get back to the stables and pick up Mandy from the café. He gave a sharp whistle and waved to Sawyer, who was riding on the other side of the herd.

Sawyer returned the wave and Brody headed in. As he unsaddled and stalled his horse once again, he thought about the attack on Mandy the night before. If it had been somebody snooping around for cash or items of value, then why hadn't he turned and run when Mandy had called out? It was the question that kept going around and around in his head.

And how sure could they be that the intruder had been a man? He dismissed the idea that a female had wielded a knife and tried to get into the room where Mandy had run. She had been under the impression that the intruder was definitely a male.

Still, even though he wanted to believe that they had all overreacted the night before and Mandy wasn't in any danger, he just didn't believe it.

Something was going on...something that had killed George Wright and now threatened his daughter. But what? Was it a neighbor dispute or somebody George owed money to? And what could that person hope to gain by harming Mandy? Dead people couldn't pay debts.

It took a lot of rage to slit a man's throat. That was an up-close-and-personal kind of anger. Brody was far too intimate with that kind of rage.

He walked into the café fifteen minutes before Mandy's shift was due to end. The first thing he saw was her beautiful smile as she glanced at him. What had become a flicker of familiar heat lit in the pit of his stomach. He turned and took a stool at the counter.

Daisy sauntered over to him. "Hi, Brody. What can I get for you?"

"Just a cup of coffee, thanks."

She returned a moment later with the coffee. "Rumor has it you have a nice smile. It must be like a unicorn…elusive as hell, because I've never seen it."

Brody looked at her in surprise, and then he not only grinned, but a burst of laughter escaped him.

"Well, I'll be damned. I do believe in unicorns," Daisy exclaimed. She was still chuckling as she moved down the counter to fill another customer's cup.

Brody turned slightly on the stool so that he could see Mandy. She was serving Abe Breckenridge and his wife, Donna. She said something and the older couple laughed.

Did she know how wonderful her smile was? Did she realize how her caramel eyes snapped with a liveliness and warmth that were so inviting? Her black slacks fit like a second skin and the yellow T-shirt that advertised the café was pulled taut across her full breasts.

He'd always found Mandy physically attractive from a distance, and getting to know her had only increased his attraction to her.

Damn. He jerked his gaze to his coffee cup. He had to snap out of it. Part of the problem was that it had been several years since Brody had been with a woman. For a while he'd driven into Oklahoma City to see a woman he'd originally met in a hotel bar there while on a cattle buying trip.

Monica Blake had a ranch on the outskirts of the city. She was a widow, highly sexual and not interested in any emotional connection. It had been the perfect arrangement for Brody for about six months and then he'd stopped seeing her. The sex had become mechanical and empty and he'd decided he'd rather do without it.

Since then he'd worked hard and slept well and sex hadn't even entered his mind.

Until now.

Until Mandy.

Friends didn't sleep with friends, he told himself firmly. And Mandy would always be just a friend because he didn't do any other kinds of relationships. He was with her now only through a series of troubling events that had been out of his control.

"Hey, cowboy, are you ready to blow this place?"

Mandy's voice came from right behind him. He turned around and fell into her welcoming smile. Her scent seemed to surround him, invading his senses. He stared at her for several long moments.

"Brody?" Her smile turned into a quizzical frown.

"Yeah, I'm ready." Thankfully she stepped back so he could slide off the stool without brushing up against her.

As they stepped out of the café his gaze shot both ways, looking for any sign of approaching danger. He wasn't even sure what danger might look like, but he was determined that nobody would get close enough to harm Mandy.

He didn't breathe easily until they were in his truck and headed to her place. While he drove, she chatted, telling him about her day and who she had seen and any gossip she had heard.

"Are you in one of your moods?" she asked.

"No, why?"

"You're very quiet."

He flashed her a quick glance. "Sometimes it's hard to get a word in edgewise with you."

"I do like to talk," she agreed easily. She was silent for a moment but he felt her gaze still on him. "You know, I thought it was only women who could have resting bitch face, but you have it."

He shot her another quick glance. "Excuse me?

What is resting bitch face?" He pulled to a stop in front of the garage.

"I'll show you when we get inside." Together they got out of the truck and went up the stairs. "I hope you like chicken," she said as she unlocked the door. "I'm making chicken and rice with a wine sauce for dinner."

"Sounds good."

The first thing she did when they entered her place was kick off her shoes. "Oh, my aching feet," she said and then smiled. "One of the health hazards of waitresses everywhere."

She plugged in the small Christmas tree that sat on a small table in the living area. "Do you like Christmas?" she asked as she got busy with the dinner preparations.

"I guess it's okay," he replied without much enthusiasm.

"I love it," she said.

Normally Brody took his meals in the ranch dining room with the other men. The meals were made by Cord Culley, or Cookie as he was known, a crusty man who rarely spoke to anyone.

It was odd to be sitting in such an intimate space while a beautiful woman cooked for him. Thankfully it didn't take long for the scent of the chicken to override the fragrance of Mandy.

"I need to be at the kissing booth by seven," she said with her back turned to him. "So, we'll have to eat and run." She turned to face him. "What vegetable do you like?"

Although there was no emotion on her face, she looked slightly irritated. Had he somehow made her mad with his rather lackluster response to Christmas? "What's wrong with you? Did I say something wrong?" he asked.

She framed her face with her hands. "Resting bitch face."

"You do that pretty well," he said.

She laughed. "Not half as well as you do. Most of the time you look like you're mad at the world. Now, green beans or corn?"

"Corn," he replied. As she turned back to the oven he frowned thoughtfully. He probably did appear as if he were mad at the world. Hell, he'd been mad at it since he'd been five years old and his father had punched him so hard in the face he'd given him his first, but certainly not last, black eye.

Before he could go too deep into his dark memories, dinner was served. "Did you hear anything from Dillon today?" he asked after eating a few bites of the delicious, tender chicken and tasty rice.

"No, nothing. But Jimbo and two of his goons came in to eat and to not so subtly remind me that my dad owed him money and interest is accruing daily."

"That's not your problem," Brody replied.

"He was definitely trying to make it my problem." She stared down at her place.

"He didn't do anything to hurt you, did he?" Brody sat up straighter in his chair.

"No, he was just being his usual creepy self."

Brody focused back on the meal. If Jimbo King tried to hurt Mandy in any way, then Brody would unleash the deep, dark rage he believed was inside him. If that happened then God help them all.

Two hours later Brody was parked in front of the kissing booth. He sat in the truck and watched as Mandy interacted with the people who passed by.

Abe Breckenridge and his wife, Donna, stopped at the booth. They all visited for several minutes and then Abe dug his wallet out of his back pocket. He handed Mandy a bill as his wife shook her head good-naturedly. Mandy grabbed the old man by his chin and then planted a kiss on his cheek.

The memory of her soft, warm lips against his skin burned in Brody's head. He wanted another kiss from her. He wanted it right now.

As Abe and his wife walked on by, he got out of his truck, the night air cold, and there was only one thing that would warm him. Just a kiss on the cheek in exchange for a donation, he thought. What harm could there be in that?

"Hey, did you get cold in the truck?" she asked, her eyes glittering in the Christmas lights that decorated the booth. "There's a little heater in the back area if you want to come in and get warm, although I'll warn you, the heater doesn't do much."

"Nah, I'm good. I just realized I hadn't donated to the cause." He pulled out his wallet and withdrew a ten-dollar bill. "Keep it all." His heart suddenly quickened as she took the money and then leaned forward.

He tipped the brim of his cowboy hat up as a wild anticipation swept through him.

She took him by the chin, and even as his mind told him to turn his head to receive the kiss on the cheek, he refused the mental command.

Her eyes widened in the instant before his lips claimed hers.

Chapter 7

Mandy gasped softly as their lips met and he wrapped his arms around her. The wooden barrier of the booth between them was the only thing that kept her from leaning fully into him as the unexpected kiss deepened.

She'd been cold with the night air slicing through her, but his lips were so wonderfully warm against hers and her entire body instantly heated. The sound of the distant Christmas carols and the bright colored lights faded away as she lost herself in the kiss.

Their tongues danced together in a heated battle that threatened to weaken her knees with desire. She had wanted him to kiss her for what seemed like an eternity and the reality was so much better than what she had imagined. A moan of exquisite pleasure escaped her.

Why was he doing this now…here where she couldn't get as close to him as she wanted? Here where it could be only a kiss and nothing more?

"Damn, that must have been a heck of a donation."

The deep, familiar voice penetrated through the haze of desire that had momentarily held her captive. She and Brody sprang apart like two guilty teenagers caught by an angry parent.

"Dillon," she said with a small shaky laugh. She shot a quick glance at Brody, wondering if the kiss had affected him as deeply as it had her.

It was impossible to tell as he eyed Dillon. He reached up and straightened his cowboy hat. "I hope you're bringing us some kind of news," he said.

"Not the kind you want," Dillon replied. "I just thought I'd let you both know that Jimbo has alibis for the night of George's murder and last night. On both nights he and his employees were playing cards in the back room at the pawn shop. We have also spoken to Aaron Blair and Lloyd Green today. Aaron was at home with his wife last night and Lloyd was in bed with the flu."

"None of those alibis sounds very ironclad to me," Brody replied.

Dillon nodded. "I realize that and we're working to see if any of them don't hold up under closer scrutiny."

"What about Nate Coleman? You mentioned my father had fought with him," Mandy asked.

"Nate has been a bit uncooperative. He's a bull-headed man and is offended that we'd even consider him a suspect. Have you remembered anything else about the person who attacked you last night?"

"No, nothing." She didn't want to tell him that she'd spent the entire day and evening consciously not thinking about the attacker. Even now, remembering those moments shot an icy blast through her that had nothing to do with the weather. "Although I'm pretty certain it was a male by his height and build."

"I just want to assure you that I'm doing everything I can to solve not only your father's murder but also to find the person who came after you. We'll get to the bottom of this, Mandy." Dillon's eyes were lit with determination. "We need more time."

"I know, Dillon," she replied.

"We'd just like the answers sooner rather than later," Brody added.

"I'll keep you informed of the investigation's progress," Dillon said and then, with a nod, he walked away.

Mandy turned to gaze at Brody. She didn't want to talk about the attack. She wanted to talk about the kiss they'd just shared. More than anything she wanted to repeat the kiss.

"You've still got about an hour left. I'll be in the truck." Before she could say a word to Brody, he turned and hurried to his vehicle.

She released a deep sigh and tried to tamp down the emotion his kiss had wrought inside her. There was no way it had been just an accidental meeting of lips.

If that had been the case then he'd have immediately pulled away from her, but instead he had deepened the kiss. He'd wrapped his arms around her like he'd meant it.

It had been more than a little bit wonderful and marked a definite change in their relationship, a change she welcomed. There was no question he was feeling some sort of desire for her. Was he the toad she'd been waiting for? She wasn't sure, but her heart quickened at the possibility.

She smiled as she saw her brother and Zeke Osmond approaching the booth. She was happy to see Graham even if she wasn't thrilled about the company he kept.

"Hey, Mandy. Don't you look cute," Graham said with a warm smile.

"Sexy. She looks sexy as hell," Zeke said.

Graham elbowed him hard in his side and Zeke yelped. "That's my sister you're talking about," Graham said. "Have some respect."

"Jeez, you didn't have to break my rib," Zeke whined.

"Are you making lots of money for charity?" Graham asked.

"A dollar here, a dollar there. Every little bit helps," she replied.

Graham pulled out his wallet, withdrew a twenty-dollar bill and handed it to her. "I always like to help a good cause."

"Thanks, bro," she replied and then looked pointedly at Zeke. With obvious reluctance he took out his wallet and handed her a five.

"I'll take four ones in change," he said.

Graham rolled his eyes as Mandy counted out the dollar bills into Zeke's awaiting hand.

"I paid a dollar. Don't I get a kiss?" Zeke asked and stepped closer.

Ick, Mandy thought as she leaned forward and gave him a quick peck on the cheek. "Did you know your buddy Lloyd is a suspect in my father's murder?" she asked.

"Lloyd wouldn't kill anyone, especially over a two-hundred-dollar debt," Zeke scoffed. "Besides, on the night of your dad's murder, Lloyd was with me and a couple of the other men having a barn party with pizza and beer."

She didn't know whether she could believe a single word that fell out of Zeke's mouth. She looked at her brother once again. "Do you want to meet me at the house tomorrow around six?"

"Sure," he agreed easily. "It would be nice if I could help you get everything done there before I have to head back home."

"I really appreciate the help, Graham, and I'll see to it that you get your inheritance once the ranch sells."

"I'm not worried about that. Maybe this spring I'll come back to visit and bring my fiancée with me. I can't wait for the two of you to meet. I know you're going to like each other."

"When are you planning on getting married?" Mandy asked.

"We've been dating for the past five years. I already feel married, but she wants the ring and the ceremony, so we're kind of planning a wedding sometime late in the summer."

"When that happens I hope I'm invited," she said.

Graham gave her another smile. "I wouldn't have it any other way."

"Come on, man. I'm freezing," Zeke said and stomped his feet. "This reunion stuff might be heart-warming for the two of you, but it's not doing anything to keep me warm."

"Mandy, I'll see you tomorrow at the house," Graham said, and then the two headed down the sidewalk.

The streets were deserted and Mandy was more than eager to talk to Brody about that kiss. Even though it was a little bit early, she closed down the awning. She stepped into the small back area and turned off the heater and the lights, then locked the place down and hurried around the building to Brody's truck.

Thankfully he had the engine running and heat spewed from the vents. "I didn't realize how cold I'd gotten until now." She held her fingers up toward one of the vents.

"What did your brother and Zeke have to say?" He pulled out of the parking space and onto Main Street.

"Zeke told me Lloyd is innocent and has alibis, and my brother is planning on meeting us tomorrow night at the house," she replied.

"Those Humes men are thick as thieves and this wouldn't be the first time they lied to alibi one of their own," he replied.

"I don't believe anything any of them say. I hope you don't mind going back to the house with us tomorrow night," she said.

"For the time being, your schedule is mine."

She wanted to talk about the kiss, but he appeared distant and unaccountably tense. His gaze remained solely focused on the road ahead and his fingers clenched and unclenched around the steering wheel.

She glanced out the passenger window and then looked back at him. "I wonder if we'll have a white Christmas."

"I'd be happy if it didn't snow for the rest of the year, although we do need the moisture."

"I suppose snow makes your job at the ranch more difficult."

He merely nodded his head. Once again she stared out the passenger window and they drove the rest of the way to her place in silence.

Was he sorry about the kiss? Had he found it horrible? Nobody had ever complained about how she kissed before, but that didn't mean Brody had found it pleasurable.

"Do you want me to turn on the television?" she asked once they were inside and settled in for the night.

"Only if you want to watch it," he replied.

"Are you hungry? I've got some apple pie in the refrigerator."

He sat at the kitchen table. "That sounds good. Apple pie runs a close second to my favorite pie of all time."

"And what's that?" she asked curiously.

"Cass used to make an awesome pecan pie. I don't know what her recipe was, but I've never tasted better."

"How about a cup of coffee to go with your second favorite kind of pie?" she asked.

"Sounds great."

"Coming right up," she said, pleased to have something to do.

Things were awkward again between them. She knew why, and sooner rather than later they were going to talk about it. She cut him a large slice of the pie while a short pot of coffee dripped into the carafe. When the coffee was ready she served him and then sat opposite him at the table.

She waited until he'd taken several bites. "Brody, we need to talk about it."

He looked up from the plate and set his fork down. "There's nothing to talk about. It happened, it's over and it's not going to happen again." His stoic gaze dared her to continue the conversation.

She drew in a deep breath. As far as she was concerned there was lots to talk about and she wasn't going to back down from having a conversation he obviously didn't want to have.

Brody had known at some point or another she would bring up the kiss. Damn that kiss. It had rocked him all the way down to the tips of his cowboy boots. And that was why it couldn't ever happen again. The very last thing he wanted was to talk it to death over a piece of apple pie. He just wanted to forget all about it.

She was silent as he finished his pie and coffee, and he thought he was going to get his wish. He got up and carried his dishes to the sink, where he rinsed them and put them into the dishwasher.

"Don't you think it's time to call it a night?" he asked as he turned back to face her.

She got up from the table and walked over to the sofa. She sat and crossed her arms. "We aren't calling it a night until we talk about the kiss."

She might be as friendly as a puppy, but at the moment she looked more like a stubborn junkyard pit bull. He bit back a sigh of frustration. "I don't understand what there is to talk about. We kissed. It was no big deal."

Hurt leaped into her eyes. Although he hated to see it, hated even more being responsible for it, better she be hurt over a kiss than something worse.

"You didn't feel anything special when we kissed?" she asked.

Brody was not a liar, but if there was ever an occasion to become one, this was it. "Special? Nah, it was pleasant enough but I wouldn't say it was anything special."

"Pleasant," she echoed flatly.

He gave a curt nod. "And in any case, friends shouldn't kiss."

She wasn't satisfied with his answers. He could tell by the way she jumped up off the sofa and stalked over to her dresser. She grabbed her pajamas out of a drawer. "I'm taking a shower," she said and then went into the bathroom and slammed the door behind her.

Crap, what did she want from him? She knew he

didn't want anyone in his life. Wasn't it enough that he'd stepped up to be her friend? To be her protector?

Did she really want him to tell her that the kiss had been special? That it had sizzled a fire through his entire body? That it had left him wanting more... oh so much more? What good could come from that?

He placed his gun on the coffee table and then got comfortable on the sofa. Maybe the best thing for him to do was pretend to be asleep when she got out of the bathroom.

That was exactly what he did. She exited the bathroom and the lights turned out. The scent of her candles filled the room and after several minutes of complete silence, Brody fell asleep.

He awakened just before dawn and remained on the sofa. Immediately his thoughts went back to the kiss and the conversation that had followed.

Would she still be irritated with him this morning? It didn't matter. In fact it would make this whole thing a little better if their relationship didn't feel quite so easy.

An hour later she awakened with a smile on her lips and apparently no hard feelings. They shared coffee and talked about the schedule for the day, and then he dropped her off at the café and headed on to the Holiday Ranch.

Despite the cold he was looking forward to riding in the pasture and smelling cold country smells instead of the sweet, hot scent of her.

But before he could get outside, he needed to check in with Cassie to make sure there was nothing pending that he needed to see to in his acting role as foreman.

He parked in the shed designated for personal vehicles and then walked the distance to the big two-story house. It was late enough that he knew Dillon would have already left for his office in town.

The Holiday Ranch was a large operation, specializing in grass-fed Angus beef. Pastures stretched as far as the eye could see. Outbuildings dotted the landscape, some big, some smaller. The largest building was the cowboy motel, that housed a dozen men in reasonable comfort.

It was amazing to think about all the changes on the ranch over the past eight months, starting with the spring tornado that had killed big Cass Holiday.

Her death had been mourned deeply by the men who had grown up under her tutelage. She'd been boss, mother and champion to them all. She'd left the ranch to her New York City niece, and for months the men had all worried that Cassie Peterson would sell the place off and return to the big city.

The storm cleanup had resulted in the men tearing down a damaged shed, and it was then the skeletons of seven young men had been discovered.

Ranch foreman Adam Benson had not only been responsible for all those deaths but had also killed a newly hired ranch hand. He had then set his eyes on killing Cassie.

Luckily Dillon had stopped Adam with a bullet that had killed him, and Cassie had fallen in love with Bitterroot and ranch life and Dillon Bowie. The future of the ranch was no longer in question.

The workforce at the ranch had changed, as well. Some of the cowboys had found love and moved on. New men had taken their places. For Brody, this was the only place he intended to live for the rest of his life. This was home in a way no other place had ever been.

He knocked on the back door and Cassie greeted him, ushering him into the large, airy kitchen and offering him a cup of coffee. Minutes later they were seated at the table.

"How's Mandy?" she asked.

"She's holding up remarkably well under the circumstances." He had to admire how Mandy had refused to allow the attack on her to change the way she was living her life. Of course, his presence made that easier for her, but he had a feeling she would have responded the same way even if he wasn't in the equation.

A shadow darkened Cassie's bright blue eyes. "You do know Dillon takes each and every crime in this town personally."

"Trust me, I know," Brody said drily. "It's tough to be on Dillon's suspect list."

"The problem is he has too many suspects in the case of George's murder," she replied.

"And no suspects when it comes to Mandy's attack."

Cassie nodded and tucked a strand of her shiny blond hair behind one ear. "You just make sure you keep Mandy safe. She seems like a real sweetheart."

"That's my plan," he said.

For the next fifteen minutes or so they discussed ranch business. "Cassie, I don't know how long this thing with Mandy is going to last. Maybe it would be best for you to pick another man as foreman," he said.

"Absolutely not," she replied. "The men all respect you, and you have all the skills I want in a man who is overseeing things. Right now it isn't necessary for you to be here every minute of every day. You take care of Mandy and we'll talk later about the foreman job if it becomes an issue."

Knowing they were finished, he rose from the table, thanked her for the coffee and then stepped back out into the clear morning air.

He headed straight for the stables. Inside the tack room Sawyer Quincy was cleaning saddles and Clay Madison sat on the end of a sawhorse. "Hey, Boss," Clay greeted him. "Nice of you to make it into work so late in the morning," he said with good-natured sarcasm.

"Ha. At least when I'm here at work, I actually work," Brody replied.

Clay stood and patted Sawyer on the back. "I just thought he could use some supervision." Sawyer snorted and rolled his eyes.

"So, how goes it with you and Mandy?" Sawyer asked.

"It goes," Brody replied.

"You two getting real close?" Clay asked with a knowing lift of one of his blond eyebrows.

Brody scowled. "Not that way. She needs a friend right now and that's all I'm being for her."

"That apartment where she lives looks pretty small," Clay pressed.

"And I'm sleeping on her sofa. I know it's tough for you to realize that a man and a woman can share space without any sex being involved."

Clay laughed. "I see my reputation as a womanizer is slightly exaggerated."

"Don't you have something to do besides supervise Sawyer and needle me?" Brody looked pointedly at the door.

Clay laughed again. "Okay, guess I'll go help Mac and Flint work on the broken mower."

"That man needs a good woman to tame him down," Sawyer said once Clay had left.

Brody laughed. "The problem is he has too many good women on the chain."

There was no question Clay had a reputation as the town's Romeo, and the bewildering thing was that no woman he'd been involved with came away disliking him.

"I'm going to head out to the pastures," Brody said.

Sawyer nodded. "Then I'll see you at lunch."

The day passed far too quickly and before Brody knew it, it was time to head back to the café. He and Mandy had agreed that they would eat dinner there before heading out to meet Graham at the house for more packing.

He arrived at the café with a curious mix of dread and anticipation. He hated that he looked forward to seeing Mandy, but the truth was he was eager to see that warm, wonderful smile of hers directed specifically at him.

Twenty minutes later she sat in a booth opposite him as they waited for their orders. "Whew, it's been a busy day and my feet are killing me," she said.

"Sorry about your feet," he replied and looked out the window. "It's unusual for us to not have snow on the ground this time of year, and with Christmas only ten days away I'm sure everyone is enjoying being out and about."

"What do you want for Christmas?" Her eyes sparkled as she gazed at him.

You. The word leaped into his mind unbidden and a swift irritation filled him. "I don't believe in getting or giving gifts," he replied. "As far as I'm concerned, Christmas is just another day."

She frowned at him. "You sound just like my father. That's what he always said. You're just a Grinch. Didn't you all celebrate the holiday when Cass was alive?"

He definitely didn't like being compared to George. Before he could answer, their meal arrived. He'd ordered the roast beef special and she'd ordered a burger and fries.

"Cass always joined us in the cowboy dining room for a special Christmas meal, but we never exchanged gifts," he said once the waitress had left.

"This year things are going to be different," she said as she picked up a french fry and dragged it through a pool of ketchup. "Christmas Eve day I have to work in the morning, but I'm off at two. When I get home we'll bake cookies and watch Christmas movies. Then on Christmas day I'll invite Graham over for a big meal, we'll listen to carols and it will be a wonderful Christmas. You're going to enjoy it."

"You're getting kind of bossy," he replied with a small smile.

She grinned. "A woman has to do what a woman has to do. Now, we'd better eat so we aren't late to meet Graham."

A half hour later they were back in the truck. "I called Seth earlier today and told him he could pick up some of the furniture at six thirty tonight," she said.

"I'm sure he appreciates any donations you might give him."

"There are only a few personal items I want to keep, mostly things that belonged to my mother."

He shot her a quick glance. "You have good memories of her?"

"A few. Mostly when I think of her I think of music and the scent of jasmine, and I feel warm and loved. What about you? Do you have happy memories of your mother?"

His fingers tightened on the steering wheel. "My mother was nothing more than a shadow who drifted from place to place in the house, trying to not get hit."

Mandy released a small gasp. "Your father hit her?"

"He didn't just hit her. He beat us both. I think my mother died because it was the only way she knew to finally escape him."

"Oh, Brody." She reached out and touched his shoulder. The warmth of that soft touch penetrated through his jacket and made its way straight to his heart.

The conversation angered him. He wasn't mad at her, but he hadn't intended to share the information, and now his head was filled with old memories that stirred a familiar anger inside him.

His father throwing a dinner plate at the wall while his mother cowered in a corner... Brody being told to clean up the slop his mother had cooked. Never knowing when a fist would slam into him, or when a kick would take him down. Never knowing any safety at all.

By that time they'd reached the house, where Graham's rental car was already parked. He exited his car as they got out of Brody's truck.

"I'm all ready to work," he said with his wide smile.

"Me, too," Mandy replied. She led the two men to the front door, unlocked it and then ushered them inside.

"Maybe we should try to finish up Dad's bedroom?" Graham said.

"That's probably a good idea," Mandy replied, but a shadowed darkness leaped into her eyes. Brody knew she was probably remembering the last time she'd been in that bedroom, desperately trying to keep the door closed against an attacker with a knife.

He hated that memory in her brain. He wished he could erase it from her mind. But he couldn't do that, so instead he slung his arm over her shoulder and they all moved down the hallway. She leaned into him as if aware of his emotional support.

They worked together boxing up books for the library and clothes for a local charity. They tossed away items that had no value to anyone. There was a drawer full of paperwork that looked to be important. Mandy dumped it in a box to take back to her place and look through at another time.

At six thirty Seth showed up with a couple of young men and a huge truck.

"I can't thank you enough," he said to Mandy as his men carried out the sofa and then came back in for chairs and other furniture.

"I'm just glad you can use everything," she replied. "I was going to donate the beds to the thrift store unless you want them."

"I'll be glad to take them. Those are the kinds of things I store, and as some of the younger folk start setting up housekeeping, they know they can come to me for help," Seth replied.

It was an hour later when Seth drove away, and the house now held a vacant echo. Mandy walked around the nearly empty room where her father had slept. "I still can't believe somebody killed him," she said softly.

"I always thought I'd have the chance to come back here and make peace with him," Graham replied, a wistfulness in his tone. "I hate it that I waited too long."

The siblings hugged and then stepped apart. "Are you sure there isn't something you want to keep from here?" Mandy asked him. "I'm planning on keeping a few of Mom's things unless you want them."

Graham shook his head. "I don't want anything. Are you going to do anything before putting the house on the market? Several of the bedrooms could use a coat of paint."

Mandy shook her head. "No, I just want to be done with it. The only thing I need to do is look for a place for me to move. I'm hoping the apartment above the garage will be a good selling point."

"It's a decent place with good land," Brody said. "You shouldn't have any problem selling it, but it might not be before spring."

"Dad still had a small mortgage on it, but we can pay that off and still have a bit of money to split," she replied.

"I've told you I don't care about the money," Graham replied. "Take it and open that restaurant you've talked about. And now, I think I'm going to take off. I'm not used to moving furniture. I didn't realize I was so out of shape."

Mandy turned to Brody. "If you don't mind, I just want to grab a few things from upstairs and then we can call it a night."

"Fine with me," he replied.

Goodbyes were said. Minutes later Graham left and Brody followed her up the stairs. They had gone up only halfway when frantic yelling came from outside.

"Stay here," Brody said firmly. He turned and flew back down the stairs and out the front door with his gun drawn. It took a moment for his eyes to adjust to the darkness. When they did he saw Graham on the ground next to his car.

"Help me," Graham moaned and slowly pulled

himself to his feet. Brody gasped at the sight of blood trekking down his chin from a busted lip.

"What happened?" Brody asked as he holstered his gun and ran to him. He held Graham up and helped him back toward the front door.

"Somebody attacked me." Graham moaned again and leaned heavily on Brody. "I thought he was going to kill me." He spat a mouthful of blood. "He came out of nowhere. I think he might have broken my ribs."

They reached the front door, and in the better lighting Graham's wounds became more apparent. He not only had a busted lip but also showed the beginnings of a swollen, blackened eye.

"Mandy," Brody called. "We need to get your brother to the emergency room."

She came running down the stairs and cried out as she saw Graham. "Oh my God...what happened?"

"We can talk on the way. Let's go," Brody replied.

They got into Brody's truck, and as he drove Graham told Mandy what had happened. "Whoever it was, I thought he was going to kill me. He punched me in the face first and then, when I fell on the ground, he kept kicking me and kicking me." Graham's voice trembled slightly and his breathing was labored.

Brody remained silent, but a cold chill took possession of his body. George had been murdered and somebody had attacked Mandy. He suspected that same somebody had gone after Graham. It appeared that person wanted to wipe the entire Wright family off the face of the earth.

Chapter 8

Mandy paced the emergency waiting room, fighting back tears as they waited to hear about Graham's condition. Dillon had already arrived. He'd questioned her and Brody and then had gone to speak to Graham.

Who had done this? Who had attacked her brother? What in the heck was going on? Not only was she now afraid for Graham, but this had also brought back her fear for herself.

Was this a warning to her? Maybe Jimbo King reminding her about the debt? Or was it something else altogether?

"Mandy, come sit down," Brody said and patted

the plastic chair next to where he sat. "You're wearing a hole in the floor."

She walked over to the chair, sank down and then looked at him through tear-filled eyes. "Brody, why is this all happening?"

His eyes were soft. "You know I don't have an answer for you." He threw an arm around her shoulder and she leaned into his solid warmth.

Usually whenever he had his arm around her and she smelled his familiar scent, she somehow believed everything would be okay. But at this moment, she wasn't sure how anything was ever going to be okay again.

She squeezed her eyes tightly shut, trying not to think of how horrendous Graham had looked, attempting not to remember all the blood that had been on her father.

Who was it? Why were they after her and her brother? What did they want?

Her eyelids shot open and they both stood as Dillon came back into the room. The man looked ten years older than he had the last time she'd seen him. This little crime spree or whatever was taking its toll on him.

"How's my brother?" Mandy asked. "They haven't let us back to see him yet."

"The doctor is on his way out momentarily. I'm headed out to your place to take a look around," Dillon replied.

"I hope Graham was able to give you more information than he gave to us," Brody said.

"The attack came out of nowhere. The man wore a ski mask and ran off when Graham managed to cry out for help." Dillon sighed. "Not much to go on."

"But it sounds like the same person who came after me," Mandy said.

"Except whoever it was beat your brother. Thank God he didn't have a knife or we'd be having this conversation downstairs in the morgue."

Dillon's words shot a new chill up Mandy's spine. Reality had become a nightmare and the only thing that kept her from spinning into complete insanity was the man standing next to her.

The man whose kiss had sparked a life, a desire inside her that no man had ever done before. At the moment it felt as if that kiss had happened a lifetime ago.

Dillon said his goodbyes, and then Dr. Wendall Johnson came out and told them they could see Graham. Mandy hurried toward the cubicle where a curtain was drawn.

Mandy pulled it back and gasped at the sight of her brother. He looked small in the hospital bed. Not only was his lower lip split, but he also had a swollen black eye that looked horrendous.

"Oh, Graham," she exclaimed and moved to his side to take his hand in hers.

"It's okay, sis," Graham replied with a crooked smile. "Right now it looks a lot worse than it feels."

Dr. Johnson stepped into the small room. "Good news. Your ribs are bruised, but not broken. There's a prescription for some pain pills waiting for you in the hospital pharmacy."

"That's definitely good news," Graham said with a laugh and then winced and grabbed his side. "My ribs sure feel broken."

"Mandy and I will walk down and get your script," Brody said. "And then we'll take you back to your car or on to the motel if that's what you want."

A little over an hour later, Graham drove away from the ranch, and Brody and Mandy locked up the big house and headed for her apartment. Once inside with her coat off, Mandy collapsed on the sofa. Brody hung up his coat and then sat next to her.

"I didn't even think about Graham being in any danger," she said as a new shiver raced through her. "Thank God you heard him cry out or he might have been beaten to death."

Brody frowned. "Maybe this isn't about the debts your father owed. What happens to the ranch if you and Graham are both dead?"

She looked at him in surprise. "I guess at this point the bank that owns the mortgage would take it back. Why? What are you thinking?"

"Nothing specific. I'm just wondering if there's

somebody who wants this place badly enough to kill for it."

"But almost everyone in town knows I'm getting it ready to put on the market," she countered. "Whoever wants it can buy it from me without any blood being spilled."

Brody's frown deepened. "I just can't understand why anyone would murder your father and then go after both you and Graham." He released a deep sigh and his frown disappeared. "Hey, where's that big Mandy smile?"

"Right now I don't feel like I'll ever smile again," she replied.

"You know, it's possible Dillon has a better handle on all this than he's told us. He tends to play things close to the vest."

She eyed him skeptically. "Are you just saying that to get me to smile?"

He lightly touched the tip of her nose. "I don't want you to be afraid, Mandy. Graham is a big boy. He's now on notice and will be very aware of his surroundings until he goes back home to Dallas. As for you, as long as there is breath in my body, nobody is going to hurt you."

His eyes filled with a dark fierceness. He jumped up and walked over to lean against the kitchen counter. "It's late and you have a morning shift."

The closeness she'd felt to him only moments be-

fore was gone. He appeared distant—closed off—
and she wasn't sure what she had done.

"Did I do something to make you mad?" she
asked. "Sometimes I can do or say something really dumb and don't even realize it."

"Why do you do that?"

She frowned in confusion. "Do what?"

"You aren't dumb or stupid, but you say you are
all the time. I think you're damned smart."

She paused, for a moment captured in old memories of hurtful comments from the man she had
longed to make proud. "I've heard how dumb I am
from the time I was ten until my father died. I guess
I have an internal voice that repeats all those things
to me."

Once again Brody's eyes darkened. "My father
beat me with his fists. Your father beat you with
his words, but one was just as bad as the other. You
need to stop listening to that inner voice. You are not
dumb or worthless or anything like that, Mandy."

A wealth of emotion pressed tight in her chest,
making it impossible for her to reply. Nobody had
ever said those kinds of things to her before and she
hadn't realized until now how badly she'd wanted,
she'd needed to hear them.

"Now it's late and you have an early shift tomorrow. I suggest we get to sleep." He straightened from
the cabinet.

She nodded, still too gripped by his words to

speak. She got up from the sofa, grabbed her night-clothes and then went into the bathroom.

It was minutes later, when she was in bed and listening to Brody's deep breathing as he slept on the sofa, that she realized she was falling hopelessly in love with a man who insisted he wanted to be only her friend.

Brody drove down Main Street, looking forward to seeing Ellie again. He had so much to talk to her about and he always felt better after seeing her.

Tomorrow was Christmas Eve day and Mandy had already told him they were going to watch movies and bake cookies for Santa after she got off work. She'd also made good on her plan to invite Graham to join them for a big holiday lunch.

The bad girl of Bitterroot continued to surprise him with her warmth and happy nature. She continued to draw him to her, and he kept up his fight against his off-the-charts desire not only to make love to her but also to keep her in his world.

She made him laugh. She was so easy to talk to and she was so caring. Her domesticity made him think of everything that had left his life when his mother had died. And as always, thoughts of his mother—and his father—tightened his chest with an emotion so huge it frightened him.

At least some good things were happening. Graham's wounds were already starting to heal, and over the past couple of days they'd managed to clear out most of the rest of the things from the big house. A For Sale sign now decorated the front yard.

Unfortunately, Dillon seemed to be spinning his wheels when it came to solving George's murder and the attacks on Mandy and Graham. He'd interviewed all the likely suspects like Jimbo King, Lloyd Green and the neighbor, Aaron, but according to the lawman the interviews hadn't yielded a thing.

Nate Coleman had been taken off the suspect list when he finally showed Dillon proof that he and his wife had been in Oklahoma City visiting family on the night George was murdered.

Who was responsible for this madness? It was a question that whirled around in Brody's head at any given moment. As he thought of Mandy so terrified on the floor in George's bedroom, that same emotion filled him...one that he refused to identify but knew wasn't good.

The sun was warm, but the air was frigid as he parked at Ellie's and got out of his truck. He walked around the back of the small, neat ranch house and knocked on the back door.

As he waited for Ellie to answer, some of the tension that had been with him for the past week or so fluttered away. Seeing Ellie and talking to her always brought a little peace to his mind.

She answered the door with a smile and ushered him into the kitchen. "Coffee?" she asked.

"No thanks. I'm good."

He followed her into the living room, where he sat in a brown leather recliner and she sat opposite him at a small, feminine desk.

Ellie Miller reminded Brody of big Cass. Like Cass, she was a widow, and Brody guessed she was in her seventies. She might be older, but her sharp blue eyes behind her wire-rimmed glasses appeared to be able to look into your very soul. Brody had been seeing her in her official capacity as a psychologist for the past six months.

Nobody knew he came here. Ellie was his private relief...and his secret shame.

"So, tell me how things are in your world," she said to begin the session.

For the next forty-five minutes Brody talked about the murder and the attacks and about Mandy. He told Ellie about his anger toward George and the way he had talked to his daughter. He spoke about his wrath toward the person or persons responsible for the fear that lit Mandy's eyes.

When he was finished he was wrung out yet relieved. Ellie leaned back in her chair. "Have you told Mandy you're in love with her?"

Brody stared at her in stunned surprise. "I'm not in love with her," he finally protested. "I'm just being a friend for as long as she needs me." Dammit, there was no way he'd allow himself to be in love with

Mandy. He'd never allow himself to be in love with anyone.

Ellie took off her glasses, laid them on the top of the desk and then reached up and stroked her hand through her thick gray hair. "Brody, I feel like I'm taking your money under false pretenses."

He frowned. "What are you talking about?"

"You keep telling me about this rage issue you have, but you've never hurt anyone or destroyed property. You've never kicked a dog or outwardly displayed that your rage is out of control."

"But what about how I feel when I think of my parents? My chest fills with so much anger I feel like I'm going to explode."

"Of course you have some anger inside you, but anger can also mask many other emotions. I've told you before what I believe. Some of that particular emotion inside you isn't anger at all. It's the hurt of a little boy who never got the love he needed, the love he deserved. And you deserved love, Brody."

Yes, she'd told him that before, but he didn't believe it. He hadn't had nor did he ever want the love of anyone. "What about how I feel about the person who attacked Mandy? That's a hell of a lot of anger."

"And justified," Ellie replied with a nod. "Somebody tried to do harm to the woman you care for. The fierce male protective quality goes all the way back to caveman days."

She sighed and looked at him kindly. "All I'm

saying, Brody, is you keep talking about the monster inside you, but you're thirty-three years old and that monster has never reared its head. I can't ethically continue to take your money for a problem I don't believe you have. You're a good man, Brody. Go out and find your happiness."

Minutes later Brody was back in his truck and headed to the café to pick up Mandy. This was the first time one of his sessions with Ellie had left him unsettled. They had come to an agreement that he wouldn't see her once a week like he had been doing, but rather on an as-needed basis if he believed he was spiraling out of control. He just hadn't been ready to stop seeing her altogether.

He parked and entered the café, the scents of Italy hitting his nose. They were running a spaghetti special tonight and the whole place smelled of garlic and onions and a rich tomato sauce.

He and Mandy had already talked about eating dinner in the café before heading to her place. Daisy led him to a booth and told him Mandy had one more table to finish up and then she'd be free to join him.

Mandy came out of the kitchen and his heart did an unexpected flip in his chest. He thought of what Ellie had said and told himself it was nothing but lust that moved him where Mandy was concerned. He loved her as a friend and he lusted for her as a man. Nothing more.

He watched her covetously as she strutted over to

a booth where Butch Cooper and fellow ranch hand Luke Stillwell sat. Mandy gave them their tab, and Luke must have said something funny because she threw back her head and laughed.

Butch watched her intently. Butch...her previous boyfriend and a man Brody believed was still in love with her. Butch hadn't even been on the radar as a suspect, but should he be?

Was it possible Butch had killed the man who verbally and emotionally abused the woman he loved? Had he gone after her with a knife just to frighten her and hoped that she would turn back to him in her time of fear and need?

Was Butch that devious?

Brody didn't know if he was thinking crazy or not, but the direction of his thoughts caused his hands to clench and his stomach to tighten.

Had it been some sort of twisted jealousy that had led Butch to beat up Graham? Had anyone checked Butch's alibis for the nights of the crimes?

The two men gave Mandy cash for the bill and then got up from the table. Brody watched them until they left the café, his thoughts still twisting and turning with supposition.

If he found out that Butch was behind the attacks, Brody didn't know what he'd do. But it wouldn't be good.

Ellie was wrong.

He had major anger issues that had been bred into

him. That was what he worried about—his control snapping and becoming his father and hurting anyone he might love.

And this was why it was so important that he go through life alone.

Chapter 9

Mandy changed into her Mrs. Santa costume in the bathroom at her apartment, and even though she hadn't minded working the kissing booth, she was a little bit glad tonight was the last night.

Brody had been unusually silent as they'd eaten dinner and a shadowed darkness had claimed his eyes once again. She'd asked him if something had happened during the day to upset him, but he'd replied that he was just tired.

A wave of guilt now worried through her. Of course he was tired. Not only was he working full days on the ranch whenever she was at the café, but then she'd been working him to death at the house with all the packing. He was sleeping on a sofa and keeping a watchful eye on her at almost all times. It was no wonder he was tired.

She should let him go. Send him back to his ranch and his own life. The very thought caused a wild sense of dread to fill her. Was it so wrong of her to want him here with her? Was it wrong of her to need him to protect her against whoever might try to do her harm? Was it selfish of her not wanting to tell him goodbye for so many reasons?

She left the bathroom and sat across the table from him. "We have about thirty minutes before we need to leave. Would you like a quick cup of coffee?"

"That sounds good," he replied. "You sit tight and I'll make it." He jumped up and moved in front of the counter.

"Thanks. You know my feet always hurt after a long day at the café."

"They're going to hurt worse by the end of the night," he replied and turned to the counter.

She watched him and wondered what it was about Brody Booth that made her want him more than she'd ever wanted a man in her entire life.

Most of the men she'd dated had been relatively uncomplicated. Brody was so much more complex and that intrigued her. She thought it might take years to unravel all the threads that made him the man he was. And the idea of having that kind of time with him excited her.

Moments later he was back at the table and they each had a cup of coffee before them. "Tell me about Butch Cooper," he said.

She sat up straighter and eyed him in surprise. "What about him?"

"Did you know he's still in love with you?"

She wrapped her fingers around her mug and frowned. "I knew when I broke up with him his feelings for me were much stronger than mine for him. That's why I decided to end it. I didn't want to lead him on when I knew he wasn't the prince I was waiting for. Why? What does he have to do with anything?"

"I don't know," he replied.

She stared at him and a new rivulet of shock flowed through her. "Surely you don't think Butch has anything to do with my father's murder and everything else."

"I'm just looking at this from all angles," he replied.

"What possible angle could you be looking at that involves Butch being guilty of anything?"

"Maybe he killed a man who was mean to you." He paused to take a sip of his coffee. "Maybe he thought if he isolated you, if he made you afraid, you'd run back to him."

"That sounds like something ripped from a tabloid headline," she scoffed.

"But it does happen. I'm not saying he's guilty. All I'm saying is we can't afford to overlook anyone."

"What if it isn't any of the suspects Dillon is looking at? What if it's somebody not even on our radar?" She worked to keep her voice even, not showing the fear this whole conversation evoked in her.

"It doesn't matter. I don't intend to let anyone get close enough to hurt you." Once again that fierce darkness filled his eyes, along with what appeared to be a raw hunger.

It was there only a moment and then gone, making her wonder if she'd imagined it.

He drained the last of his coffee and then stood, his face betraying no emotion. "It's time to head into town and get you to the booth."

She quickly finished the rest of her coffee. Together they grabbed their coats and walked down the stairs to the truck.

"I'm sorry if I upset you with the discussion about Butch," he said when they were underway.

"You didn't upset me. You surprised me. I guess I'm not as much of a devious thinker as you are."

In the light of the dashboard his smile was beautiful. "I didn't know I was devious until I met you."

"Ha. So I bring out that quality in you?" she asked lightly.

"You bring out lots of qualities in me," he replied, not taking his gaze off the road ahead.

"Like what?"

"I never wanted to get rid of my resting bitch face before I met you."

She laughed, delighted by the sense of humor that shone from his eyes as he flashed her another quick grin. "What else?" she asked.

He looked back to the road. "You bring out the protective caveman in me."

"I like the protective part, but I'm not so sure about the caveman thing," she replied. "If you ever grab me by the hair and try to drag me anywhere, we're going to have a problem."

He laughed, that deep, wonderful rumble that made her want to fall into his arms. "I don't see me doing anything like that soon."

As always driving down Main Street into Bitterroot proper filled Mandy with a sense of pride and belonging. There were only two long blocks of businesses, but in those two blocks was a lot of heart.

There were no empty storefronts or going out of business signs. Instead there was a vibrancy to the town. They passed the busy mercantile store and Brody parked directly in front of the booth, where Janis Little, a bartender at the Watering Hole, was offering up kisses to passersby.

"I'll see you later," Mandy said and then got out of the truck and hurried around to the back of the booth to enter. The little heater couldn't compete against the cold night air that blew through the wooden structure.

"Whew, I'm glad you're here," Janis said as she met Mandy in the back room. "The streets have been busy all day."

"Everyone is scurrying around to finish up their last-minute Christmas shopping." Mandy shrugged off her coat and hung it on the hook just inside the door. "Are you going home to relax or do you have to work at the Watering Hole?"

"Working," Janis replied and pulled on her coat. "But at least I don't have far to go home afterward."

Mandy knew Janis lived in an apartment in the back of the popular bar. "And it's a weeknight so the bar closes earlier."

Janis flashed a smile. "Thank goodness for small favors, right? Cash box is on the shelf." She gave Mandy a quick hug. "Merry Christmas and I'll see you around."

"Merry Christmas to you, too," Mandy called after her as she exited the booth.

Janis was a couple of years older than Mandy. She was not only pretty but also nice. Mandy had spent some time visiting with Janis at the bar and she'd always admired Janis's self-confidence and sense of humor. Having her as a best friend would be a lot less complicated than Brody, she thought as she moved to the front of the booth.

From this vantage point she could see him sitting tall behind the truck's steering wheel. She waved at him and he returned the gesture.

His presence filled her not only with a sense of well-being but also with a sizzling excitement and anticipation.

She'd always been able to envision the future of owning her own restaurant. She'd toyed with a menu and experimented with food. She'd also been able to visualize being happy in the role of business owner. But no matter how hard she tried she couldn't see the future where Brody was concerned.

She was in love with him. She believed he was the prince she'd been waiting for, but if he didn't want her to be his princess, then she couldn't see how they would continue a friendship for any length of time when this was all over.

Shoving these thoughts out of her mind, she pasted on a friendly smile as Dr. Dan Richards, the town vet, and his wife walked toward her. "Hey, Doc and Michelle," she greeted them.

"Hello, Mandy," Dan replied. "How are you doing?" His voice held a touch of sympathy.

"I'm getting by. How is business?" she asked.

"A little slow this time of year, but I'm looking for homes for a few cute puppies."

Mandy held up her hand. "Don't even tell me about them. I have too much on my hands right now to try to take care of anything."

"Could you put the word out?" Michelle asked and handed her a five-dollar bill.

"Sure, I'd be glad to." She took the bill Michelle proffered. "Do you want a kiss?"

Michelle laughed. "No, I think we can skip that part of this."

"Thanks for the donation."

She visited a moment longer with the two and then they continued on their way.

She was grateful that for the next hour she kept busy, talking to fellow townspeople and adding to the cash for the youth group. Occasionally she stepped into the back room to stand for a few minutes next to the heater. She noticed Brody starting his truck now and then and knew he was also seeking some warmth in the cold winter night.

A moan of dismay escaped her as she saw Zeke Osmond, Lloyd Green and Shep Harmon approaching. They all looked half-drunk, laughing and elbowing each other as if they were a bunch of teenagers. The muscles in her stomach knotted. This was the first time she'd have any interaction with Lloyd, another man her father had owed money to.

Before they reached the booth, Brody got out of his truck. He didn't approach her or the booth. He merely leaned against the driver's door with his arms crossed in front of his chest, a reassuring, totally hot presence.

"I see you've got your junkyard dog nearby," Zeke said as they stepped up in front of her. The other two men guffawed as if he'd just spoken the world's most humorous line. Mandy didn't laugh. She couldn't even work up a fake smile.

She'd never liked or dated any of the men who worked for Raymond Humes. She'd always found them rude and distasteful. She disliked them even more now that Brody had told her about how much trouble they all had caused over the years on the Holiday Ranch.

"I want one of those hot kisses of yours," Zeke said as he pulled his wallet out of his pocket.

"I think I should get one for free since your daddy owed me money," Lloyd added. Lloyd was an older man. Mandy would guess him to be in his late forties or early fifties. She'd never seen him when he didn't look scruffy and tonight was no different. He was badly in need of a haircut and shave and his black coat was covered with hair and hay.

"I don't give away any of my kisses for free," she replied curtly.

"That's not what I heard about you," Zeke said, and once again they all laughed and nudged each other.

"Make your donation and move on," she said, fighting against the old hurt of her blackened reputation.

She cast a quick glance at Brody. He immediately unfolded his arms and took a step forward. She shook her head to keep him in place. The last thing she wanted was for these creeps to provoke a street fight.

Zeke gave her a dollar and she leaned forward and quickly kissed his cheek. The other two didn't offer up any money and she sighed in relief as they sauntered on down the sidewalk.

Once they were gone Brody walked over to her. "Are you all right?"

"I'm fine," she replied. "They're just a whole lot of nastiness."

"They work for a man who is worse than nasty. Raymond once tried to rape Cass when she was taking care of her sick, dying husband." He grimaced as she gaped at him in shock. "I shouldn't have told you that."

"I won't tell anyone," she replied. "Do all the men at the ranch know about it?"

"No, I think I'm the only one Cassie told. If some of the others knew they'd kill Raymond without blinking an eye."

"You said he tried to rape her, so I'm guessing he wasn't successful?"

A small smile curved the corners of his mouth. "He was not only unsuccessful, but she delivered a snap of her bull whip on his bare ass that apparently scarred him for life."

"Good for her," she replied. "And don't worry, I know how to keep secrets." Their conversation was cut short as another couple approached.

Brody looked at his watch. "You have about a half hour left. I'll be in the truck."

Fifteen minutes later Butch showed up carrying a shopping bag in one hand. Mandy greeted him with a smile, but she remembered Brody's crazy idea about the tall, handsome cowboy. Was it really so crazy? Was it possible Butch was capable of doing such things?

"Last-minute shopping?" she asked.

"Yeah. At least I didn't wait until tomorrow night. On Christmas Eve the stores are packed with people who put off shopping until the last minute." His gaze was warm...too warm as it lingered on her. "If things had worked out between us I would be buying something special for you."

"But things didn't work out," she replied firmly. "I hope you find the woman who will be your everything, Butch."

"I thought I'd already found her," he said. He shrugged and offered her a sad smile. "I just hope Brody is making you happy."

"He is," she replied even though that wasn't exactly true. Butch didn't have to know that what would really make her happy was if Brody would kiss her again. She wanted him to take her to bed and make love to her... That would make her beyond happy.

"I hear tonight is the last night for this particular money drive." Butch pulled out his wallet and handed her a twenty-dollar bill. She leaned forward but he shook his head. "I'm good without the kiss."

"Thanks, Butch. You know Seth appreciates

every dollar. I hope you have a wonderful Christmas," she said.

"Thanks, and the same to you. I'll see you around." He turned and walked back the way he had come.

She watched him, wondering how she had missed that he was apparently still crazy about her. How crazy was he? Crazy enough to slash her father's throat? Devious enough to attack her and then beat up Graham?

She pushed away these troubling thoughts as the minutes wore on. Several other people stopped to donate and chat. At five minutes until nine she decided to shut down shop. The streets had emptied and she was more than ready to go home and get off her feet.

After waving to Brody, she pulled down the awning and secured it. She unplugged the Christmas lights and stepped into the back room.

She didn't see him in the semidarkness. She had no warning at all. A body slammed into hers and gloved hands wrapped around her throat and squeezed so tightly she couldn't scream... She couldn't even make a sound.

She thrashed and kicked in an attempt to get him away and off her. Her fingers scrabbled at his gloved hands in an attempt to dislodge his hold from around her throat. Air...she needed air.

With no success, she tried to poke her fingers into the eyes that stared at her through the ski mask slits.

She attempted to raise her knee up to hurt him, but he held her too tightly against him.

Brody, help me, she cried in her mind. He was so close...just outside in his truck, but he might as well have been a thousand miles away. She wanted to cry, but she had no breath. She couldn't fight because she had no strength left.

Her lungs began to burn with the desperate need for oxygen. She had no idea who he was. The man was killing her. Dark shadows flirted around the edges of her vision.

She was dying.

That was her last thought. Then the darkness claimed her.

Brody tapped his finger a bit impatiently against the steering wheel, wondering what was taking Mandy so long. Usually once she closed the awning it only took her a minute or two to reappear from the back of the booth. Tonight it seemed to be taking her much longer. He waited another couple of minutes and then got out of his truck.

"Mandy?" he called out before he reached the booth's back door. He rounded the corner of the structure and a man in a black coat and a ski mask exploded out of the door and took off running in the opposite direction.

Shock swept through him. Although he wanted to chase after the bastard, instead a panic made his heart race as he thought of Mandy. He hurried into the booth as a sense of horrendous dread filled him.

The dread was realized as he saw Mandy lying still on the floor. "Mandy!" He fumbled for his cell phone as he ran to her side.

He fell to his knees beside her at the same time Dillon answered the call. "Get an ambulance to the booth. Somebody attacked Mandy and she's hurt. He's running down the back alley."

"On my way," Dillon replied.

Brody dropped the phone. "Mandy...wake up. Please wake up." Was she dead? No, she couldn't be. He refused to believe it. He placed a finger on her pulse point in her neck.

Nothing. Oh God, he felt nothing. Guilt and grief surged up inside him. No. This couldn't be happening. They hadn't thought about the booth's back door. He hadn't considered that anyone would be bold enough to attack her here with him just outside.

He moved his fingers frantically against her skin—bright red skin—desperate to feel a pulse of life. He had no idea what the man had done to her. He saw no blood that would indicate a wound, but he was afraid to move her to check for injury to her back.

There! A faint beat against his fingertips. He nearly sobbed in relief. "Mandy, I'm right here. Hang on. Help is coming." He had no idea if she could hear him or not, but it didn't matter.

All that mattered was that she was still alive.

As he lifted his fingers from her pulse point, he stared at the angry redness and purpling around her neck. Strangled. His blood ran cold. She'd been strangled and there was no question in his mind that she'd be dead now if he hadn't decided to see what was taking her so long.

She moaned and her eyelids fluttered, but her eyes didn't remain open. "Mandy, you're going to be all right." He had no idea if that was true or not, but he desperately needed to believe it.

He shuddered in relief at the sound of a siren, indicating help was on its way. She moaned again and raised a hand to her throat.

"Mandy, I'm right here and you're going to be okay," he said. If he got hold of the person responsible for this, he'd beat the hell out of him. A wild anger filled him. It was the kind of rage that always frightened him...a monster's rage.

He tamped it down by drawing in deep, even breaths. The man who'd done this wasn't his concern right now. Mandy was. The siren halted and within minutes the little room was filled with EMTs and Dillon.

"I've got men checking the streets," Dillon said as they loaded Mandy onto a stretcher.

"You won't find him," Brody said flatly. "He's either long gone by now or he just removed his ski mask and went to the café for a cup of coffee," he added with a touch of frustrated sarcasm.

"I've also got men checking out the likely suspects," Dillon replied. "Do you have a description to give me?"

"Medium build, dark coat and a ski mask. If you have any more questions for me, talk to me at the hospital. I've got to go with Mandy."

The EMTs had wheeled Mandy out and all he could think about was her condition. As the ambulance drove off Brody followed right behind it, his heart beating more quickly than he could ever remember.

Would she be okay? Had oxygen been squeezed off for seconds? Minutes? Was it possible she might never fully wake up? His world would definitely be worse without Mandy in it.

Nausea rose up in the back of his throat. He was sick with guilt and fear. It was his own damned fault. He'd underestimated the danger.

He'd believed she was perfectly safe in the kissing booth with him parked right in front of it. He hadn't thought of the vulnerability of the booth's back door.

He arrived at the hospital and watched helplessly as she was whisked away into the emergency room. There was nothing he could do now but sit in the waiting room and agonize.

He was the only person in the room, and he sat for just a moment before jumping to his feet and pacing the length of the area. Had she been hurt even more seriously than he knew?

Had the man kicked her when she'd fallen unconscious? Had she been stabbed someplace where he hadn't seen? Did she have internal injuries in addition to the bruises on her throat?

His heart thundered as he waited for somebody to come out and give him an update on her condition. Minutes ticked by. He'd never been the type of man to make small talk with anyone, but how he wished Mandy was at his side right now, chatting about who she'd seen at the café that day.

She challenged him to engage in conversations about everything and nothing. He hadn't had any real laughter in his life before her and he damned straight wasn't ready to tell her goodbye yet.

He'd been in the waiting room alone for about forty-five minutes when Dillon walked in. "How is she?" he asked.

"I don't know. I'm still waiting for somebody to tell me something. Let me guess—you didn't find anyone," Brody said.

"You guessed right." Dillon's frustration deepened the lines across his forehead as he gestured Brody to a chair. Together they sat.

"I was hoping you might have thought of some detail, anything that might help identify the perp," Dillon said.

Brody shook his head. "Nothing, and I'm assuming you have nothing concrete to tell me."

"I can tell you Jimbo, Sean Watters and Donny Pruitt were in the back room at the pawn shop when my men checked in with them. They all said they'd been there the entire evening."

"They would alibi each other and there are a million places to hide a ski mask in the pawn shop," Brody said. "I know it wasn't Jimbo because of his size, but either one of the other two could have attacked Mandy and still have time to get back to the pawn shop before you checked on them."

"I also checked in with Graham even though he's really not a suspect anymore. He was in his motel room and I'm waiting to hear back reports on some of the others."

"Whoever it is, he's like a damned ghost, striking out and then disappearing into the night. For the life of me I can't figure out why somebody wants Mandy and Graham dead. If it was just George, then I could figure he was killed by somebody he'd ticked off with his mean, big mouth."

"I've twisted this every which way possible and can't find a motive," Dillon replied.

"Have you checked out Butch Cooper?"

Dillon looked at him in surprise. "No, why?"

"He was at the booth minutes before Mandy was attacked." Brody went on to tell him what he'd been thinking about the tall, cowboy as a vengeful ex-boyfriend.

"I'll check it out," Dillon replied and then frowned. "Whoever attacked her tonight took a huge chance. It was one hell of a bold move. It speaks of an urgency that's definitely worrisome."

Worrisome? Hell, it was a lot more than that to Brody.

"He's attacked her twice unsuccessfully. He's going to be angry and that will only make him more dangerous," Dillon continued.

Before Brody he could reply, both men stood as Dr. Johnson came into the room. "How is she?"

"Her throat is bruised and it's going to be sore for several days, but she's conscious, alert and asking to get out of here."

Brody nearly sagged in relief. "Can I see her?"

"Examining room four," the doctor replied.

Brody exploded through the doors that led to the emergency patient rooms. All he wanted to do was see her, assure himself that she was really going to be okay.

He found her room and stood in the threshold. A small light shone over the bed, highlighting the shiny strands of her long, dark hair. She had her eyes closed and appeared to be resting peacefully.

Still, every muscle in his body clenched painfully tight as he continued to gaze at her. Her beautiful, slender throat was nearly black with the bruising. God, he'd almost lost her. It had been such a close call.

Her eyelids flickered open and she smiled. It was the most beautiful smile he'd ever seen. "I didn't mean to wake you," he said.

"You didn't. I wasn't sleeping. I was just resting with my eyes closed."

Her voice was slightly raspy, and knowing what had caused that rasp only tightened his muscles more. He took several steps closer to her. "I'm sorry, Mandy. I'm so damned sorry I let you down."

"Stop it," she replied. "No Brody-bashing allowed."

"I need to be bashed," he replied. "I should have thought about the vulnerability of the booth's back door."

"The booth is now history. All I want to do now is get out of here and go back home." She raised a hand to her throat and winced.

"Are you sure you're okay to go home?" he asked worriedly.

"My throat hurts, but other than that I'm fine. The doctor said I could be released and all I want to do is get into my own bed."

She gestured for him to come closer and then grabbed his hand. Hers was cold and quivered slightly. He squeezed her hand, hoping to reassure her.

At that moment Dillon walked into the room. For the next few minutes he questioned Mandy. She wasn't any help in identifying who had attacked her. But as Brody listened to her recount the attack, his rage grew. He flashed back to a vision of his father... face red and muscles bunched. The man slammed a television remote control against Brody's head and then beat him with his fists when the batteries came loose in the remote.

Brody had been about six and his father had beat him from the living room and into Brody's bedroom. There had been no help from his mother, who was afraid her husband would turn his wrath on her.

Max Booth had been a monster and his blood ran through Brody's veins. Ellie hadn't seen it and nobody else seemed to understand Brody's fear that somehow that monster would be unleashed. It was what frightened him more than anything in his life other than the attacks on Mandy.

Dammit, he'd hoped she was dead when he ran from the booth, but now he wasn't so sure. He'd seen the ambulance arrive from his hiding place in the shadows of the night.

Now he sat in his car on a dark stretch of a country road, angry that he hadn't had another minute or two to ensure that she was good and dead.

Thank God her boyfriend had been more worried about her condition than chasing him down. The last thing he wanted was to end up behind bars. Been there...done that.

He stared at the burner cell phone on the passenger seat. His boss would be waiting to hear from him and he hated like hell to tell him he'd failed once again.

His boss was already ticked off that he hadn't managed to stab her to death when he'd entered her father's house and she'd been there all alone. Who would have thought she'd possess the strength to keep him out of the bedroom?

He hated the taste of failure in his mouth. It had been easy to slit the old man's throat. He'd been surprised and pleased that the front door hadn't been locked. He'd been even more pleased to find George sleeping in his recliner. George hadn't even opened his eyes as he'd drawn his knife across his throat.

Mandy was another matter. One failed attempt to kill her was bad. Two was untenable. Oh yes, his boss was definitely going to be pissed.

All he could do was call him and try to smooth things over. He had to let his boss know that one way or another Mandy would not live to see the New Year.

Chapter 10

It was a little after midnight when Brody and Mandy finally left the hospital. There was a full moon overhead and the sky was a blanket of shiny stars.

"It's a beautiful night," she said once they were in the truck and headed home.

"Thank God you're here to enjoy it." He shot her a quick glance. "You seem to be handling everything remarkably well for a woman who was nearly strangled to death."

"All's well that ends well, right?" she replied lightly. "I'm just ready for bed now."

He had a feeling she was in some sort of shock and once that shock lifted, her real emotions would set in. When that happened it was possible she'd be angry with him for not protecting her. He'd accept her anger because he more than deserved it.

What he wouldn't do was allow her anger to chase him away. She was stuck with him until Dillon got the bad guy in jail. There was no way he intended to walk away from her now when she needed him more than ever. He didn't give a damn how long it took. He intended to be by her side until all danger to her had passed.

She was quiet for the rest of the ride home and he didn't prompt her to speak. Her throat had to hurt. She had to be exhausted from the trauma and hopefully she'd feel better after a night's sleep.

Once they were inside her place, she grabbed her pajamas and headed into the bathroom. Brody sat on the sofa as she took a long shower.

He couldn't believe how lucky they had been. There was no doubt in his mind that if he'd waited a couple more minutes to see what was taking her so long, she'd be dead. He couldn't even begin to process the loss of her.

He jumped up when she emerged from the bathroom, smelling fresh with that hint of brown sugar and vanilla that he always found so appealing. Damn those pajamas that fit her just tight enough to encourage him to fantasize about her body beneath them. She appeared so soft...so touchable. His fingers itched with the need to reach for her. "Ready to sleep?" he asked instead.

She nodded and climbed into her bed. He walked over to the side of her bed and picked up the candle lighter. With a flick of the trigger he lit the candles that she always slept with.

"I'm going to take a shower. Will you be all right?" he asked.

Once again she nodded, and then she closed her eyes. Brody went into the bathroom and took a shower. As he lingered beneath the hot spray, he tried not to think about the attack and how she must have felt.

But it was difficult not to think about it. She had been terrorized. She'd believed she was going to die. He couldn't imagine the level of fear she'd experienced when that man had been squeezing her throat and she couldn't draw any air.

Brody would have given anything to take that experience away from her. He never, ever wanted her to feel that kind of pain, that kind of terror again.

He got out of the shower, redressed in a clean pair of jeans and a pullover shirt and then left the bathroom.

He assumed she was asleep as he eased down on the sofa and closed his eyes. He was almost asleep when she called out his name. Instantly he was awake.

"Can I get you something?" he asked.

"Could you just come over here and hold me for a few minutes?"

Her husky voice trembled and held a wealth of need. He found it impossible to deny her comfort after what she'd been through. She'd been so strong up until now, and it appeared she was finally feeling the aftermath of her near-death experience.

He got off the sofa and walked to her bedside. Even though he knew it would be tough for him to hold her body against his own and not want her, he told himself he could be strong for the both of them.

She raised the sheet to allow him to slide in next to her, and he noticed that tears glistened on her cheeks. Compassion swept through him and he gathered her into his arms.

Her pajamas were snuggly soft, her body warm as it curled against his. She hid her head in the side of his neck and clung to him.

A swift surge of desire exploded through his veins. He desperately tried to tamp it down as he stroked her hair and attempted to comfort her.

"Don't cry, Mandy. It's over now and you're safe." Her hair was silky soft and he continued to touch the long strands.

"I was so scared," she said, her breath a warm caress against the underside of his jaw. "I couldn't breathe and I thought he was going to kill me."

"Thank God he didn't." He stroked a finger down

her cheek, the softness of her skin once again stoking a brighter-burning fire inside him.

"I tried to fight him off, but he was so strong and his hands around my neck were so tight. I tried poking him in the eyes, but nothing I did stopped him from strangling me. I was so afraid I was going to die in that kissing booth. I was terrified that I was going to die before you and I got a chance to make love."

He froze, certain that he must have misunderstood her. She raised her head and looked at him, her beautiful brown eyes filled with a longing that half-stole his breath away. "Please, Brody, make love to me tonight."

He knew he needed to get up. He needed to get out of the bed and away from her immediately. This would be wrong on so many levels. But instead he found his lips on hers, and someplace in the back of his mind, he knew he was lost.

Her mouth was hot and welcoming. Still, in a last-ditch effort to regain control, he tore his mouth from hers. "Mandy, this just isn't a good idea."

"It's a wonderful idea. No strings, Brody. I don't and I won't expect anything from you. Just give me tonight and make love to me." Her arms pulled him closer...close enough that their mouths met once again.

She deepened the kiss, swirling her tongue against his in an erotic dance that fully aroused him. His heartbeat accelerated as wanton lust swept through him.

He'd desired her long before their vehicles had collided in the snowstorm. Each day since then his desire for her had only increased and now it was as if he'd wanted Mandy Wright all his life.

As the kiss continued, he ran his hands over the back of her pajamas and then across her breasts. Her nipples were hard against the soft fabric and that only excited him more.

They kissed for several minutes longer and then she plucked at his shirt. "Take it off," she whispered. "I want to feel your bare skin against mine."

He didn't wait for her to ask him twice. He sat up, pulled his shirt over his head and then tossed it to the floor next to the bed.

When he turned back to her, his breath caught in his throat. She'd taken off her top, as well, and the flicker of the candles played on her full bare breasts. She looked stunning in the soft illumination.

He took her lips once again and rolled her over on her back as his hands covered her breasts. He ran his thumbs across her turgid nipples and she released a deep moan.

He slid his lips down the length of her neck, careful to avoid the bruised area around her throat. He nipped and kissed softly across her collar bone and then captured one of her nipples between his lips.

She placed her hand on the back of his head, as if

to encourage him as his tongue swirled around the taut peak. He stroked down the length of her, the heat of her body radiating through her pajama bottoms.

His jeans had grown painfully tight with his full arousal. He wanted to be naked, and he wanted her naked and gasping beneath him.

After kissing her one more time, he slid off the bed. He stood and unbuckled his belt, then took off his jeans, leaving him clad only in a pair of boxers.

Their gazes caught and held for a long moment. Hunger. He saw it shining from her eyes and he couldn't help the surge of the same emotion that filled him. Then she wiggled beneath the sheet and he knew she was taking off her pants.

He stripped off his boxers, crawled back into the bed and then once again pulled her into his arms. His skin loved hers and the familiar scent of her made him half-wild.

Another husky moan escaped her as he stroked across her breasts, down the flat of her stomach and then to her inner thigh.

She arched her hips and he touched the very core of her, using his fingers to bring her pleasure. He was more than ready to take her but he wanted her to reach her peak before he indulged himself in her.

"Brody," she half growled his name, hands grasping his shoulders. Tension filled her body and he moved his fingers faster, more frantically. Her eyelids fluttered. She stiffened and then cried out his name once again as shudders went through her.

"Now," she said. "Please, take me now, Brody."

He moved into position between her thighs and slid into her. He trembled and lost all conscious thought at the exquisite pleasure of her heat surrounding him, but he was barely inside her. He pushed in harder and encountered some resistance. He pushed again and she cried out. He froze as rational thought slammed back into his head.

He gasped in stunned surprise and stared down at her. The bad girl of Bitterroot had been a virgin until a second ago.

"Don't stop," Mandy gasped urgently. She gripped him by his broad shoulders, knowing exactly why he had stopped. She'd wanted it to be him. She'd wanted him to be her first. "Brody, please don't stop."

He released a groan that seemed to come from the very depths of him and then stroked into her. She'd heard that the first time could be painful and, truth be told, it was a bit uncomfortable. However, the hunger that shone from his eyes, the soft groans of pleasure that escaped him, made the pain not matter.

It didn't take long before he found his release. He cried out her name and half collapsed on top of her. He was only there for a moment, and then he rolled off her, grabbed his jeans from the floor and disappeared into the bathroom with a slam of the door.

Mandy remained in the bed, preparing herself for his wrath, and there was no question that it had been anger that had driven him out of the bed and into the bathroom.

She had no regrets. Kissing him and feeling his hands all over her body had been heaven. She'd been waiting a very long time for the man she wanted to make love to her, and it had been well worth the wait. Now she was excited for them to do it all over again. It would be so much better the next time.

He came out of the bathroom, a half-naked scowling cowboy who didn't know he held her heart. "What the hell were you thinking?" he asked angrily.

"I was thinking about how much I wanted you. I was thinking that I didn't want to die a virgin," she replied.

"You should have told me ahead of time."

"If I had told you, would you have made love to me?"

"Absolutely not." He pulled out a chair at the table and turned it around to face her. He sat and glared at her. "Did I hurt you?"

"Just a little bit, but I expected it. For goodness' sake, Brody, don't look so gloomy. You actually did me a favor. You have no idea what a burden it's been to have the worst reputation in town and still be a virgin," she said lightly.

"Don't joke about it," he snapped. "You should have waited for the prince you talk about all the time.

I'm just another damned toad and you should have never given that to me." He raked a hand through his dark hair. "Hell, we didn't even use protection."

"Don't worry. I'm on the pill and I'm clean." She released a deep sigh. "You're really ruining my afterglow. Why don't we just say good-night, and if you feel the need you can scowl and yell at me some more in the morning."

"Aren't you supposed to work a shift tomorrow?" He got up from the chair and moved to the sofa.

"I already texted Daisy to tell her I wouldn't be able to come in." Now that the desire was gone from her, the burning pain of her bruised throat had roared back to life. She was also suddenly overwhelmed with exhaustion. The night had held so many highs and lows.

She got out of bed, grabbed her pajamas and walked naked to the bathroom. After dressing, she stared at her reflection in the mirror. For the first time in twenty-nine years it wasn't a virgin who stared back at her. And there wasn't an ounce of regret in her heart. She'd always believed she'd have sex for the first time with a man she loved, and that was exactly what had happened.

She knew the score, and what she'd told him about not having any expectations of him was true. The fact that he cared enough about her to be with her now was all she needed.

Even his anger about taking her virginity warmed

her heart in a perverse sort of way. It showed that he really did care about her.

Brody's eyes were closed when she left the bathroom, but she knew he wasn't sleeping. She crawled back into bed. She stared across the candlelit room for a long moment.

"Brody?" she called softly.

"What?" He didn't open his eyes.

"I was just wondering when we were going to make love again," she asked.

His eyelids snapped open, and even in the semi-darkness she could feel his scowl. "When hell freezes over. Now go to sleep."

She rolled over on her back and smiled. She could already visualize the arctic chill moving into hell. Because she'd been aware of his hot gaze on her when she'd walked naked across the floor. Because she'd felt a new hunger radiating from him even as he'd been arguing with her.

Whether he knew it or not, they were going to make love again. And she couldn't wait for it to happen again.

The man in the dark ski mask grabbed her by the throat and squeezed. *Help me*, she cried in her mind. *Somebody please help me. He's going to kill me.*

Air. She needed air. Her lungs burned and her heart felt as if it might explode in her chest. She desperately needed to breathe.

Suddenly she was released. She cried out in relief as she hit the kissing booth's floor. She breathed in precious oxygen and then looked up and saw that the man was still there, only this time he held a knife in one hand.

Run! a voice inside her head screamed. *Get up and run!* But she couldn't. In fact, no matter how hard she tried to move, she couldn't. She was frozen, no muscles responding to her inner pleas. The wicked knife gleamed as brightly as the man's eyes as he advanced toward her.

He raised the knife and she tried to scream, but nothing would come out of her throat. She didn't want to die. As the knife thrust toward her, she finally managed to scream.

"Mandy... Mandy, wake up. You're having a nightmare."

Brody's deep voice pierced through the terror, and when she opened her eyes and saw him, she burst into tears. "I was being strangled...and...and then he was going to stab me to death," she managed to gasp out between sobs.

He sat on the edge of the bed and pulled her into his arms. "Shh, it's all right," he said as she burrowed her head in the crook of his neck and continued to cry. "It was just a nightmare and you're okay."

The fear of the dream containing so much reality

continued to roar through her. Brody caressed her back and murmured comforting words.

Eventually the fear slowly dissipated and her tears turned into hiccupping gasps. She finally raised her head. "I'm sorry, Brody. I didn't mean to blubber all over you. I can be so stu..." She halted and shook her head. "You're right. It was just a horrid nightmare."

"Are you good to go back to sleep?"

Oh, when he looked at her with such caring, she could almost believe he might love her. "I'm good," she replied. He got up from the bed and headed back to the sofa. "Thanks, Brody."

"No problem," he replied.

Within minutes she was once again asleep. When she opened her eyes again, the sun was shining through the windows and Brody sat at the kitchen table with a cup of coffee. The television was on a news channel with the sound turned all the way down.

"Good morning," she said as she sat up. "What time is it?"

"Almost ten."

"Oh my gosh, I never sleep this late." She scrambled out of bed, appalled by the lateness of the hour.

"You had a pretty rough night. You deserved the extra rest. How's your throat?"

She raised a hand to her bruised throat. "Sore, but I'll survive. I'm going to take a quick shower and then I'll make you some breakfast." It was more than a little sore, but she wasn't going to think about it and she definitely didn't want to be a whiner.

"Not necessary," he replied. "I made myself a couple of pieces of toast a little while ago. I noticed you had some tea bags in the cabinet. How about I make you a cup of hot tea with some honey when you get out of the shower? It might be good for your throat."

She looked at him in surprise. "Oh, that would be so nice. I won't take long." She grabbed the clothes she intended to put on and then went into the bathroom.

Brody's tone had been civil, yet distant. She had a feeling he was still more than a little bit irritated with her. But his offer to make her a cup of tea touched her heart. She'd spent her entire life taking care of her father and herself. Nobody had ever offered to do much for her.

By the time she showered and dressed in a pair of red jogging pants and a red-and-white Christmas T-shirt, he had the cup of tea ready for her.

"I don't know if you use sugar or milk or whatever," he said. "I did put honey in it but that's all."

"A little milk would be nice." She sat at the table as he placed the carton of milk and a spoon in front of her. "I'm not used to being waited on."

He put the milk back in the fridge and then sat once again. He curled his fingers around his coffee cup. "It's nice to have somebody wait on you once in a while."

"I imagine you haven't gotten much of that in your lifetime," she replied as she stirred her tea.

"I've always taken care of myself." He picked up his cup and eyed her over the rim. "You know I'm still angry with you."

She didn't pretend not to know what he was talking about. "I don't know why you're so angry. It's my body. I decide what I'm going to do with it and I decided I wanted to make love with you."

"You should have saved your virginity for the man you're going to marry," he replied gruffly.

"Brody, I told you last night that I don't and I won't expect anything from you, if that's what has you so worried." Even as she said the words she knew he wanted to hear, they were a lie. Oh, she didn't expect Brody to feel obligated to love her because of what had happened the night before. But she couldn't help but wish that he'd fall crazy, madly in love with her.

"You're my best friend and I appreciate everything you're doing to keep me safe," she added. "What happens between the sheets stays between the sheets."

He grunted as if at least momentarily satisfied and took a drink of his coffee. "So, what's on the agenda for today?" He set his cup back down on the table.

She smiled at him. "Since I'm not working and it's Christmas Eve day, we have lots of stuff to do. Once we're finished with our coffee, first we're going to bake cookies for Santa. I usually bake at least two different kinds."

"You do realize there is no Santa," he said drily.

"It's tradition," she replied. "I always bake cookies for Santa and he gets a glass of milk, too."

"And are the cookies eaten and the milk gone the next morning?" He raised a dark eyebrow.

"No, but that doesn't matter. The spirit of giving and love is what Santa Claus is all about and so I do believe in him."

"Do you also believe in unicorns?" It was obvious he was teasing her.

"Of course. Unicorns are wonderful creatures but they're so shy they are rarely seen." She raised her chin as he released a laugh and shook his head.

"What about leprechauns?"

"Nasty little creatures who love to play games."

"You don't really believe all this, do you?"

"I believe in magic and miracles," she replied.

He stared at her for a long moment and his eyes grew darker. "You do realize that princes only show up in fairy tales."

"And I believe in fairy tales," she replied. She believed with all her heart that he was her prince. All she had to do was somehow convince him.

Chapter 11

Brody woke up just before dawn on Christmas day. He didn't get up. Instead he remained on the sofa, thoughts racing through his head…pleasant thoughts.

Yesterday they'd made and frosted cookies. Despite the trauma Mandy had been through, in spite of her bruised throat, she'd been lighthearted and fun.

Fun.

There certainly hadn't been much fun in his life up until now, but Mandy managed to pull out a happiness he hadn't known he could feel.

She'd been mentally and verbally abused by her father all her life. Somebody had tried to kill her twice, yet she had a sunny disposition and an optimism that drew him to her.

And she'd given him her virginity. Damn. It was the last thing he'd expected. Hell, who in the entire town of Bitterroot would believe that Mandy Wright had been a virgin?

She'd dated so many men. Why hadn't she chosen one of them to be her first? Why hadn't she slept with Butch, who obviously adored her? Now there was no way to go back in time and put the genie back in the bottle.

Still he had to admit there was a small part of him that was pleased he'd been her first, that liked the idea she'd chosen him.

Giving her an alibi for the night of her father's murder had bound them together, but this had bound them together even more.

He was still a little angry with her about the whole thing. He didn't deserve to be the man who'd received that gift. If he'd known she was a virgin they never would have gone there. He wouldn't have allowed things to get out of control.

But making love to her had been nothing short of amazing. She had fit so perfectly against him and the feel of her, the very scent of her had driven him out of his mind.

Just thinking about it now created a new heat inside him, a heat that both enticed and irritated him. He got up from the sofa. The candles had gutted overnight, but the faint light of dawn crept into the windows.

On the kitchen table she'd left a saucer with two frosted cookies in the shape of snowmen, a glass of milk and a note to let Santa know she'd been good.

He couldn't help the smile that turned his lips upward as he thought about the icing fight they'd had while frosting the cookies. He couldn't remember how it had begun, but they'd chased each other around the apartment, laughing and yelling like two kids.

By the time it had all ended he'd worn red and white frosting across one cheek and his forehead and she'd sported green frosting on the tip of her nose and on her chin.

He picked up one of the cookies from the saucer and took a big bite, then chased it down with a drink of the milk. Being as silent as possible so as not to awaken her, he walked over to a kitchen drawer where he'd seen some ink pens and paper.

After taking out a piece of the paper and a pen, he returned to the table and sat. He hadn't thought too much about Christmas but he now found himself sorry that he hadn't bought her a gift.

Her father was dead and he doubted that George had ever bought a gift for his daughter. She had no boyfriend who might buy her something special. He supposed Graham might bring her a gift, but Brody should have somehow gotten her something.

Thinking for several long moments, he finally decided what he could give her. He wrote on the paper, folded it tightly and placed it beneath her little tree. He then made coffee and returned to the table to wait for it to brew.

Last night after the cookies had been baked and frosted and they'd eaten a dinner of sandwiches and chips, they'd settled into the sofa to watch Christmas movies.

As *A Christmas Story* had played they'd laughed together and he'd tried not to want her again. Following that movie they'd watched *Miracle on 34th Street*. He'd never seen it before and he'd found himself oddly touched by the story of believing in somebody and taking a chance on love.

Jeez, what was wrong with him? She was messing with his head, making him want things he could never have. The small apartment was beginning to feel claustrophobic as he battled himself inside. Thank goodness Graham was coming to eat with them today. At least that might give Brody a break from his constant desire for her.

Dillon had called yesterday to check in on Mandy. He had no news to share with them about the investigation. For the first time Brody was starting to wonder how long this was going to take.

He was supposed to be the acting foreman for Cassie, and yet he hadn't been on the ranch for the past couple of days. What happened if Dillon didn't clear this up for weeks...for months?

He needed to get back to his own life and yet there

was no way he wanted to leave Mandy alone until she was no longer at risk. He didn't trust anyone else to have her back like he did.

She was his danger. Getting any closer to her was sheer madness. There was no way they had a future together. She had no idea who he was at his core... and his greatest fear was that his core was rotten.

By seven o'clock Mandy was up and busy in the kitchen. She had ordered Brody to the sofa and out of her way. The little Christmas tree was lit and carols played from the stereo.

"Once we eat whatever leftovers there are after this meal, we need to make a trip to the grocery store," she said as she placed a ham in the oven.

"By the size of that ham we'll be eating leftovers for the next month," he replied.

She laughed. "Go big or go home, right?"

He couldn't help but smile at her. "Are you always so happy?"

She gazed at him seriously. "I get sad and scared and disappointed like I imagine everyone does, but I have always believed you have a choice when you open your eyes in the morning. You can choose to be miserable, or you can choose to be happy. I try to choose happiness." She smiled. "And now it's time to get busy making my special sweet potato casserole."

At noon the whole place smelled of baking ham and cinnamon and spices and more wonderful scents that had Brody's stomach rumbling with hunger.

Under Mandy's watchful eye, he set the table for the meal, and soon after that Graham arrived.

The food was delicious and the conversation light and easy. Graham's eye still sported a faint shadow of a bruise, but that was all the remaining evidence of the beating he'd taken. They didn't talk about the attacks that had occurred or George's murder.

When the meal was over they lingered at the table over coffee. Brody was quiet, simply enjoying the laughter and chatter of the siblings.

It was good that the two had been reunited. They still had another week of Graham being here before he flew home to get back to work and his fiancée. But they made plans to visit each other often, and Graham talked about Mandy being in his wedding party when he and his fiancée got married.

At least she'd have her brother when Brody walked away from her. And he would eventually walk away, because it was the best thing he could do for her.

Once their coffee cups were empty, Mandy insisted they move to the sofa for gift-giving. Brody sat next to Graham as Mandy danced across the room to the little tree.

"Before we start…" Graham stood and pulled a small gaily wrapped gift from his pocket. "This is for you." He held it out to her.

Her eyes misted as she took it from him. "I bought you and Mom a gift every year," she said. "I wrapped them and put them under my tree and then I'd donate them to charity a day or two before Christmas. I never forgot you, Graham. I missed you every day."

Brody's throat thickened with unexpected emotion as the two hugged. Jeez, all this holiday stuff was turning him into a sappy fool.

Graham had bought Mandy a pretty gold bracelet and she gave him a bottle of cologne. Then she brought Brody a folded piece of paper he hadn't noticed was beneath the tree.

"What's this?" he asked.

"With everything that has happened, I didn't have a chance to buy you anything, so I hope you see this as a real gift."

He opened it and read. It was a promissory note for one pecan pie made from Cass's special recipe. "This is a terrific gift," he exclaimed, surprised and touched that she'd remembered a toss-off comment he'd made. "My only question is, when can I turn this note in for an actual pie?"

She laughed, her eyes sparkling with happiness. "As soon as we make that trip to the grocery store. And now...who wants a piece of apple pie?"

"Wait...you missed a present," Brody said.

She frowned and went back to the tree, where she found the slip of paper Brody had placed there earlier. She unfolded it and grinned at him. "This is the best present ever."

"What is it?" Graham asked curiously.

"It's good for five foot massages." She leaped

around the coffee table and into Brody's lap. She wrapped her arms around his neck and kissed him on the cheek. "Thank you, Brody. It's such a thoughtful, wonderful gift."

She jumped back up before he could fully register the pleasure of having her so close to him. What he did experience was an intense desire to spend each and every Christmas with her. He wanted to bake cookies and watch sappy movies with her again and again. A hungry want shot through him...the want to belong with her.

The very last thing he'd intended to happen was to fall in love with Mandy, but he had. He loved her. He was madly, crazy in love with her. And yet the odds of them being together in the future were the same as him looking out the window and spying an elusive unicorn.

Once Graham left, Brody pitched in to help her clean the kitchen. They worked in companionable silence while the Christmas carols playing from the radio continued to fill the room.

When the kitchen was back in order and the dishwasher was running, they sat side by side on the sofa. "So, what's your tradition for Christmas evening?" he asked.

"I don't have one," she replied. She could think of one she'd like to establish tonight—for them to make love again. But she knew mentioning that topic would make him mad and she didn't want to ruin what had been a wonderful day.

"Tell me about the men you work with," she said. "I can tell you what they order when they come into the café, but I don't know that much about them."

He settled back, looking comfortable and at ease. "Mac McBride often entertains us at night by playing his guitar and singing. He's also recently taken over the training of the horses and he's like a horse whisperer. And then there's Clay Madison..."

"A big flirt," Mandy said.

Brody laughed. "He is that, and then there's Jerrod Steen. He spends a lot of spare time at the youth center. Sawyer is probably the nicest guy on the face of the earth but he can't hold his liquor worth a damn. The rest of the original twelve have married and some of them have moved off the property."

"You all must have been really tight when you were growing up."

"We were like brothers." His eyes grew distant, as if he was remembering his past. "There were a lot of folks in Bitterroot who didn't look too kindly on us. Most people treated us like we were trash and probably out to take advantage of Cass. And most everyone in town thought Cass was crazy to staff her ranch with a dozen runaway boys. There was definitely an us-against-the-world mentality among us when we were all younger."

"It was good that you had each other. Once Graham ran away, I had nobody. It was hard for me to make friends in grade school because I had to hurry home from school each day to clean the house and make dinner and do the laundry."

"I'm sorry for saying this, but your father should have been shot for heaping that kind of responsibility on your head, especially when you were so young," Brody said darkly.

She shrugged. "I just thought that was what good daughters did. I guess neither one of us had a chance to have a real childhood." She didn't want to talk about her father anymore. "So, out of all the men on the ranch, who is your best buddy?"

He frowned. "To be honest, now that we're all adults, I'm not overly close to any of them. I mean, I care about them all and we have a lot of history together, but I'm pretty much a solitary person."

"Why is that?" She gazed at him curiously.

He cast a glance just over her shoulder, but his eyes filled with a shadowed darkness. "I just don't like sharing too much of myself."

Secrets. She didn't want to pry, but she wished he felt close enough to her to share his secrets with her. She wanted all of him, the good and the bad. Although she couldn't imagine that he had any bad inside him.

"I wish you could confide in me." She spoke her thoughts aloud.

"Confide about what?" he asked. He leaned forward, as if looking to flee.

"About whatever puts the shadows in your eyes. About whatever secret it is you have in your soul."

He laughed, although it sounded forced. "I think you're being a little dramatic. I don't have any big, dark secrets."

"Then why are you so afraid to have a meaningful relationship in your life?" She studied his features intently. Whether he recognized it or not, he was not only amazingly handsome but also had an intelligence that challenged her and a kindness that touched her heart deeply. Why wouldn't he want what most people did—a future filled with a real, true love?

"I like my life fine as it is," he replied, and once again his gaze didn't quite meet hers. "Marriage just isn't for me." His eyes locked with hers, and in his she saw the warning he intended.

Don't expect anything from me. Just because I'm here now with you doesn't mean I'll be here tomorrow. I'm not looking for love or marriage. Those were the kinds of words his eyes spoke nonverbally.

A sharp stab of disappointment swept through her, but she shoved it away and raised her chin. "I can't wait to be married. I'm ready to give my heart, my body and my soul to a commitment that will give me love and laughter and children."

He leaned back once again. "How many children do you want?"

"At least two—a boy and a girl—and they will know every minute of every day how very much I love them. My daughter will have the fun and free childhood that I never had, and neither of them will ever know the bite of a belt or the pain of physical or mental abuse. I hope my son will grow up to be a man like you."

He laughed again, the sound holding a touch of bitterness. "Don't wish anything about me on any kid," he replied.

"Why do you feel that way? You have some wonderful qualities," she protested. When he didn't reply, she continued, "Don't let him win, Brody," she said softly.

He frowned. "Don't let who win?"

"Your father." She scooted closer to him on the sofa. "From what you've told me he abused you until you finally escaped from his cruelty. Don't let that abuse continue to haunt you to the point that you don't reach out for happiness. Whatever loop might be playing in your head, you need to know it probably isn't true."

"Like the loop in your head that tells you you're stupid," he replied.

She nodded and then smiled. "And we both know I'm not stupid. I'm doing my best to quiet that nasty voice in my head, and you need to do the same thing."

"So noted, but that's not going to change the fact that I intend to live my life alone."

Once again a bitter disappointment filled her. She should have never allowed herself to fall in love with him. She certainly hadn't intended it. She wasn't even sure when the desire for his friendship had become something so much more, but it had exploded into a wonderful, beautiful thing.

One thing was certain. She couldn't talk him into loving her. She couldn't persuade him to want a future with her. All she could do was hold tight to the minutes they shared together right now.

She raised a hand to her throat. The soreness of the bruises would eventually heal. She had a feeling it would take her heart much, much longer to heal when Brody walked out of her life for good.

Chapter 12

The next couple of days passed excruciatingly slowly for Brody. Although he did have his days on the ranch to try to diffuse some of the sexual tension that had become a constant, tormenting companion, it just wasn't working.

Mandy certainly wasn't helping things. He believed she was being deliberately provocative when they were together in her apartment. She licked her lips far too often when eating, constantly reminding him of the hot sweetness of her mouth.

She sauntered across the room with an extra wiggle to her hips. Or was it that he was just acutely aware of her every move since making love with her?

He now raised his face to the sun as he brought his horse to a halt at the stables. It was another frigid day but the sun was bright overhead and there was no wind, making it feel warmer than it really was.

He dismounted and led his horse inside, where several other men were unsaddling to prepare to go in for lunch. He was looking forward to the noon meal with the other cowboys. It was a reminder that this was where he really belonged. Minutes later he walked with Mac McBride, Sawyer and Flint McCay into the large dining area.

Cookie had big sloppy joes, seasoned fries and a bowl of cut-up fruit ready for them.

As always there was a lot of ribbing and laughter when they filled plates and moved to the picnic tables to eat. The topic of the ribbing today was once again Sawyer's inability to hold his liquor.

"It was another stellar night at the Watering Hole," Flint said. "Sawyer had three beers and slept like a baby in the corner of the booth."

"Yeah, if we were teenagers we would have written all over his face with markers and put an alley cat on his head," Clay added.

"And even a scratching, hissing alley cat wouldn't have been able to pull him from his stupor," Flint said.

Sawyer looked sheepish. "I can't help it," he said. "I don't know why I just pass out after only a couple of beers."

"Maybe you should stop drinking altogether," Brody said.

Sawyer looked at him in horror. "But that's what we do. We all go to the Watering Hole and have a few drinks. It's been part of our tradition since all of us turned legal."

"Besides, if he didn't go to the Watering Hole he wouldn't have a chance to see his secret love, Janis." Clay grinned at his buddy.

"She's not my secret love," Sawyer replied.

"Ha! We've all noticed you looking like a love-struck teenager whenever she waits on us," Flint said.

"I do not," Sawyer protested, but his cheeks dusted with a telling color.

"Leave the poor guy alone," Brody said.

"Okay, then let's talk about you and Mandy." Clay's blue eyes sparked with a mischievous twinkle.

"Let's not," Brody replied.

"At least tell us if Dillon has any idea who's attacking her and why," Flint said.

"None that he's sharing with us." Brody's stomach knotted. "Other than the café, Mandy isn't going anywhere without me until Dillon gets somebody in jail."

"Is her brother still in town?" Clay asked.

Brody nodded. "He's got a couple more days here."

"I met him the other night at the Watering Hole. He seems like a nice enough guy," Clay said.

"Yeah, but I don't fully trust anyone after Adam fooled us all so badly," Brody replied.

The group fell silent for several long moments and Brody knew they were all thinking of the man they had grown up with, a man who had been one of their brothers and a man who was a serial killer.

Nobody had seen the malicious evil that dwelled beneath his pleasant facade. Brody had no idea who now might be hiding his rage toward Mandy beneath a pleasant face and a friendly smile.

"I still think this is Jimbo's work," Flint said. "I heard about George owing him money and this sounds like something he'd do to warn anyone else that he means business."

"Sean and Donny fit the description of the attacker," Brody said. "But so do most of the men in this town."

"I just don't get it," Sawyer said with a frown. "I mean, I get why somebody would have a beef with George, but why Mandy and her brother?"

"We don't get it, either." Brody picked up his glass of iced tea. "And believe me, we've gone over everything that's happened a hundred times."

"I hope Dillon gets on top of it soon," Mac added.

"That makes two of us," Brody replied. He had a feeling if this arrangement with Mandy went on for too long, he'd lose his mind.

To Brody's relief, the talk turned to ranch business, and the muscles that had bunched up as they'd talked about the attacks on Mandy slowly relaxed.

They tensed up again only when he was on his way to pick up Mandy at the café, and then the tension that filled him had another reason.

At least they were making a trip to the grocery store before going on home. Whenever they could spend some time outside the intimacy of the apartment, it was good. He'd rather think of buying cornflakes and milk than the wonderful silkiness of her skin. He much preferred focusing on what cut of meat to buy than how her naked body felt against his own.

It was a few minutes before four when he walked into the café. Mandy stood behind the counter and greeted him with that smile that always made him feel better no matter what had gone on during his day away from her.

"Howdy, partner," she said as he sat on the stool across from where she stood.

"Howdy, ma'am," he replied with a grin he couldn't repress. "What's cooking?"

She leaned over the counter, bringing with her that particular scent that threatened to make his head spin with desire. "Tonight's special is Daisy's fried chicken, mashed potatoes and gravy. I think we should eat here before we go grocery shopping."

"Whatever you think is best," he replied.

"I think it's best if I don't go grocery shopping on an empty stomach. Otherwise I'll fill the cart with candy and cookies and chips and dip, and that's not good for my girlish figure."

"Honey, your figure isn't girlish...it's all woman." The words fell out of his mouth before he could filter himself. He stood quickly. "I'll just go get us a booth."

"Okay, I'll join you in about ten minutes."

He turned away from her quickly, cursing himself for saying something that had put a spark of heat in her eyes. How he wanted to fall into that heat, but he refused to make another mistake with her.

But he wanted to. Their lovemaking couldn't have been that pleasant for her. She'd even admitted it had hurt a bit. He hated that. He longed to make love to her again, to teach her all about pleasure without any pain.

He'd been her first...and there was a small part of his heart that wished he would be her last. But that was crazy thinking. He couldn't allow his heart to dictate his future. He knew what he was and he'd never be right for any woman...especially one as warm and loving as Mandy.

Dillon needed to get to the bottom of the crimes sooner rather than later. Brody definitely needed to get out of that apartment and back on the Holiday Ranch where he belonged.

"Graham came in for lunch today," Mandy said when they'd been served their chicken dinners.

"Anything new with him?" Brody picked up his chicken leg and took a bite.

"He said he's been hounding Dillon for answers to the point that Dillon runs in the opposite direction whenever he sees Graham coming. Of course he was just joking about it, but I guess he's been pressing Dillon pretty hard."

"I'd be pressing him hard, too, if I thought it would make a difference," Brody replied. "But we can't wring blood out of a stone and he can't tell us what he doesn't know."

"I don't think anyone is going to have any answers until somebody tries to kill me again." A shiver of fear threatened to work up her spine. "I just hope before he gets to me, you or Dillon gets to him."

He held her gaze for a long moment. "Mandy, I've told you before that nobody is going to get close enough to kill you as long as there is breath in my body."

She believed him. She had faith in his ability to shelter her from harm. It was only one of the many reasons why she was in love with him.

For the next few minutes they ate in silence. "Tomorrow I don't work, so I'm going to make you that pecan pie," she said when they were ready to leave the café. "I asked for Cass's recipe from Cassie."

"Sounds good to me."

They walked out into the cold night and got into his truck, and as always his familiar scent wrapped around her. "I made a full grocery list during my break today."

"And do you always stick strictly to the list?" he asked.

"I always plan to, but more times than not something sneaks into the basket that wasn't on the list."

"Like what?"

"Like chocolate cupcakes or chocolate cupcakes." She laughed. "I love to bake, but there's something about those boxed cupcakes that I love. What about you? Do you have a guilty food pleasure?"

"Not really." He angled into a parking place in front of the grocery store. "The only thing I get a hankering for is Cass's pecan pie."

"And I'm going to fix that hankering first thing tomorrow," she replied.

He flashed her a smile that sparked a deep longing inside her, the longing to belong to him forever and always. She shoved it away as they got out of the truck and entered the store.

With Brody pushing the basket, they went up and down the aisles and she picked items that would ensure them at least a week's worth of meals.

"We're going to spend some time in the morning picking pecans out of the shells," she said as she placed a bag of the nuts in the basket. "And I need to pick up a bottle of bourbon. No wonder you liked Cass's recipe. It's heavy on the alcohol."

"That would explain the mellow mood I always

got after eating a couple of pieces," Brody replied with a grin.

A small fight ensued between them at the cash register when she insisted she pay for the groceries. He had done so much for her already and there was no way she was going to let him pay her for the food she cooked.

"You always pay when we eat at the café," she exclaimed. "The least I can do for you is provide you meals since you're with me to keep me safe."

She won the battle, and minutes later they were on their way home. "So, what did you do today?" she asked.

He told her about riding the range looking for broken fences that might need mending and then ordering supplies and doing the payroll.

She liked that they shared the days they spent apart, that he told her stories about the other cowboys, making her laugh, and she in turn told him about the persnickety customers she might have waited on that day.

She also loved that she thought she could tell him anything, that she could bare her entire soul to him and he'd take good care of it. Even with somebody trying to kill her and her father being murdered, she'd never been as happy as she was with Brody.

And she was going to be devastated when he left her.

She couldn't imagine loving another man half as much as she did him. She could only wish that he'd love her half as much back. There were times when she believed she saw a wealth of love shining from his eyes, but it never lasted long and she wondered if it was only lust.

Lust. She'd seen it in men's eyes from the time she was twelve and had fully developed. Lust was what she was certain drove half the men in town to ask her out for a date.

But Brody was different, she told herself. He'd cared about her as a friend first, and that mattered to her.

Still, lust was on her mind when they arrived home. It chased her as they put the groceries away. Thoughts of lust and death continued to plague her as they settled onto the sofa to watch television.

She hadn't wanted to die a virgin and she'd desperately wanted Brody to be her first. Now she didn't want to die having just one experience with making love and she desperately wanted Brody.

There was no question that since the night of the attack in the kissing booth, her own death had been on her mind. Despite Brody's protection she feared that the danger would find her.

When she thought about dying so young, she grieved for the love she would never know, the children she would never have and the sadness of her own life interrupted.

As a crime drama played on television, she kicked off her shoes and took off her socks. As usual her feet ached from standing on them for most of the day and then she thought of the Christmas promissory note Brody had given her.

"I think I'm ready to cash in on one of those foot rubs," she said.

"Feet hurting?" he asked.

She nodded. "As usual."

"Then give me your feet and tell me if I'm doing it wrong, because I've never rubbed anyone's feet before."

She turned her body so she could lift her feet up and into his lap. Thank goodness the polish on her toes was still pretty and pink.

He picked up her left foot and began to massage the bottom. His touch was light as if he feared pressing too hard might hurt her. "You can put a little more muscle into it," she said.

"Just let me know if I hurt you." He applied more pressure to the ball of her foot, and she closed her eyes and released a small moan of pleasure. It hurt some…but it hurt so good.

He massaged each and every inch of her foot and then rubbed her toes one by one. It was heavenly. "Okay, now the other foot," she said half-drowsily.

She dropped the massaged foot to his lap and realized he was aroused. Her drowsiness snapped away, and while he massaged her other foot a sense of sweet anticipation filled her.

No matter what he said to the contrary, he wanted

her. If all he had to give her was his lust, then she would take it and hope that lust would eventually drive him to love her.

She wiggled the foot in his lap. His gaze shot up and locked with hers. "What are you doing, Mandy?"

"Trying to seduce you, but I've never seduced a man before. You have to tell me if I'm doing it right."

He stopped his massage. "Mandy, you seduce me when you don't even know you're doing it."

"I do?" She looked at him in surprise.

He began to knead her foot again. "You seduce me when you smile or when you laugh. You seduce me with your thoughtfulness and with that little moan you just made. You have me crazy with wanting you."

"Then why aren't we together in bed right now?" she asked half-breathlessly.

"Because it isn't a good idea."

"Who made you the judge of ideas? Why can't we make love again? It's not like I'm a virgin," she said jokingly.

She pulled her foot from him, sat up and then scooted closer to him. "Brody, I can't tell you how badly I want you." She threw an arm around his neck and sat on his lap.

He made a half-hearted attempt to get her off, but before he could accomplish his goal, she kissed him. And he kissed her back.

"Mandy," he murmured as his lips finally slid

from hers and instead trekked down the length of her neck. "This is a mistake on so many levels."

"It's a mistake I'm willing to live with." She leaned back from him and stripped off her T-shirt.

His eyes lit, and he picked her up and carried her to the bed. Within minutes they were both naked and beneath the sheets. They moved together with frantic need. Their foreplay was hot and his mouth seemed to touch everyplace where her sensations went wild. He brought her to orgasm and it didn't take her long to want him inside her.

This time when he took her there was no pain... only waves of pleasure that had her mindless. She'd never known the height of ecstasy he evoked in her was possible. She'd never dreamed she could feel so completely connected to another human being.

As he stroked into her she raised her legs and wrapped them around his hips, taking him in as deeply as possible. He moaned his pleasure and as he stiffened with his release, his gaze locked with hers.

In that moment Mandy felt more loved than she knew she would ever feel again, with his body united with hers and the light of love shining from his eyes.

Later, when he left the bathroom and headed for the sofa, she stopped him. "Brody, please sleep with me. Otherwise I'll just feel like a booty call and nothing more."

He hesitated for a long moment and then got into bed with her. He pulled her against him and began to stroke her hair. His soft caresses felt heavenly, but she also felt the tension in his body.

"Brody, nothing has changed between us. I still expect nothing from you. I'm just grateful you're here now with me." Her heart longed to say so much more. Words of love trembled on her lips, in her heart, but she was so afraid to speak them out loud.

His body slowly relaxed. "You do realize this is just going to make things more difficult for us when I get back to my own life."

"I know," she agreed. "But can't we still be friends when this is all over?" She wasn't even sure if it was possible for her to be his friend and not want more of him. But the idea of losing him altogether was just too much to bear.

He sighed, his breath a warmth against her neck. "I'll always be around if you need a friend."

Her heart ached more than a little bit. Now would have been the perfect time for him to tell her he loved her. Now, with them naked beneath the sheets after sharing the greatest intimacy a man and a woman could share.

Instead his words had promised nothing, not even a real friendship. In all her daydreams about a prince, it had never occurred to her that once she found him, he wouldn't want her.

Chapter 13

Mandy sat in the break room in the café, eating a late lunch. Yesterday had been a nice day despite Brody being a little too quiet.

She'd not only made him his pecan pie but also cooked a nice dinner of roast, potatoes and yeasty rolls. It had been magical to awaken in his arms yesterday morning, with his warmth and scent surrounding her.

All too quickly he'd gotten out of bed. She'd hoped to spend all the remainder of their time together with him in her bed at night. But last night he'd insisted he return to his place on the sofa to sleep. It had definitely felt like a step back in their relationship.

"How's life treating you?" Daisy asked as she came into the room and took a chair at the table across from Mandy.

"Okay, although I think you enjoy the minutes of your day more when you believe death could find you at any moment."

"Jeez, girl, that's a hell of a way to exist," Daisy replied. "So, Dillon still hasn't come up with any suspects?"

"Oh, we have plenty of suspects. We just can't figure out who is guilty." Mandy pushed her plate aside. "And how is life treating you?"

Daisy released a deep sigh. "To be honest, I'm tired. I could have retired two years ago and I keep wondering if it's time to start taking it easy. I've got a nice nest egg and could travel. Maybe go on one of those cruises to Italy and hook up with a sexy Italian." Her eyes twinkled merrily. "It's more likely I'd spend my time in a lounge chair with a fistful of those fruity drinks."

"If you ever really decide you want to sell this place, let me know. Once my father's ranch sells I'll have some cash and should be able to get a loan," Mandy replied.

Daisy's red eyebrows danced up in surprise. "I thought you wanted to open your own restaurant."

"Let's face it, Daisy. Bitterroot has enough restaurants and I'd love to own this café." Already her mind filled with some of the changes she would make, mostly introducing new things to the menu, which hadn't been changed for years.

"All right, then I'll keep you in mind when that time comes. I'd like the new owner to be somebody who is passionate about food and friendly service. You definitely fit the bill."

"Thanks, Daisy. I appreciate it."

For the remainder of time she had left on her break, Mandy imagined what it would be like to own the café. She wouldn't change the cheerful yellow vinyl booths or the wall decor that just made people feel good when they entered. The bathrooms were also in good shape.

The only room she might update a bit was the kitchen. She could buy a nicer grill and offer additional menu items that were a little lighter in calories. She just hoped Daisy was serious about possibly selling in the near future.

Ten minutes later, still warmed by her boss's words, Mandy returned to the floor. It was just after one, still almost four hours before Brody would be there to pick her up. At least she wasn't working the dinner rush hour that always started just after five.

When she'd put on the shoes she always wore to work that morning, Brody had eyed the black shoes with the three-inch heels and told her that her feet wouldn't hurt so bad if she wore more sensible shoes.

"I'll wear sensible shoes when I'm sixty," she had

replied. "I won't care about fashion when I'm that old." He'd merely rolled his eyes, making her laugh.

The lunch rush was over and there weren't too many diners still seated. Mandy got a broom from the back room and began to sweep up the crumbs that had hit the floor through lunch.

She was excited about the possibility of Daisy finally retiring and her being able to buy the café. Daisy had spent years and years of her life making the café the most popular place to eat around the area.

It made much better sense to take over a success than to start from scratch. Buying the café would fulfill one of her biggest dreams. She could only wish that she had a man who loved her by her side. She could only dream that somehow Brody would be that man.

After cleaning up the floor, she put the broom away and went back out front. She wiped down the tables in her section and straightened salt and pepper shakers. She made sure the tops were screwed on tight because there was always a wise guy who thought it was funny to unscrew them and ruin somebody's meal.

Julia Hatfield was doing the same kind of housekeeping in her section across the room. Behind the counter, Trisha Cahill was also straightening and cleaning before the dinner rush began.

Trisha had married Dusty Crawford in a private

ceremony about two months before. Dusty worked with Brody on the Holiday Ranch. Mandy could only hope to follow in her footsteps, having the café as her work and Brody continuing his work on the ranch.

Abe Breckenridge and his wife walked in with their grandson, Harley, between them. The boy had gotten into trouble not long ago. He and some of his friends had broken into the convenience store in the middle of the night and had stolen a bunch of liquor. Dillon had figured out who was responsible, and although the owner of the convenience store hadn't pressed charges, Harley had been in hot water with Abe and Donna since then.

None of this was public knowledge, but Mandy had heard it from Butch, who worked on the Breckenridge ranch. Butch...was he the person who had murdered her father in a twisted way to make her life easier?

Had his love for her become so warped that he had tried to kill Graham and now wanted her dead because she hadn't run back into his arms? It was hard to imagine, but she knew Brody was right... those kinds of horrible things happened in real life.

She certainly didn't want to believe it. Although he hadn't been the prince she'd been looking for, she genuinely liked Butch. He was a nice guy and someday he'd make some woman a wonderful husband... if he wasn't a murderer.

A shiver raced through her. She'd tried to keep

thoughts of a killer out of her mind. The bruising around her throat had faded to a faint yellow and she didn't want to dwell on such negative thoughts.

But fear crept up on her in unexpected moments. She'd be pouring a cup of coffee for a customer and suddenly fighting a nauseating terror. Looking at her reflection in the bathroom mirror as she got ready for the day, she'd be overwhelmed by the horror of never seeing her reflection there again. And in the minutes before she fell asleep, she would wonder if she'd wake up the next morning or be killed.

One of her worst fears was that the killer would attack Brody and kill him. If that happened she wouldn't care if she lived or died. The last thing she wanted was for Brody to become collateral damage in a game of death she couldn't begin to understand.

"Abe, Donna, how we doing today?" she asked.

"Doing fine," Donna replied.

"And what about you, Harley? Enjoying the holiday time off from school?"

"It's okay," he replied.

"He'd like it a lot better if his grandma and me would let him run wild like half the other kids his age in town," Abe replied with a stern look at his grandson. Harley's face turned red in response.

It was almost two thirty when her brother came in. The Breckenridges had left and the café was quiet. He hurried toward her, a wide smile on his face.

"Mandy, you have to come with me. I need to show you something."

"I can't just leave. I'm working, Graham. Can you tell me what it is?" she asked.

He shook his head, his eyes glittering brightly. "It's a wonderful surprise, Mandy. It will only take a half hour at the most. Surely Daisy will let you off for that short time." He looked around. "Besides, this place is dead right now."

"This can't wait until I get off?" What did he want that couldn't wait?

"I need to show you now. Mandy, it's going to blow your mind." Graham grabbed her hand and squeezed tight. "Come with me."

"I need to talk to Daisy," she said, a bubbling excitement rising up inside her. What on earth could he have to show her that would be such a wonderful surprise? Was it something that might solve everything? Oh, that would be great.

Graham released her hand and followed her across the floor to speak with Daisy, who was seated behind the counter, reading the morning newspaper while sipping on a cup of coffee.

"Daisy, I want to steal my sister away from here. I swear I'll drop her back off here within a half hour or so. Can I steal her away?"

Daisy frowned. "This is something that can't wait for her to get off work?"

"It is," Graham replied. "Half an hour...you have my solemn promise."

"All right, go on then," she said to Graham and then looked at Mandy. "I'll see you back here in half an hour."

Before she could respond, Graham grabbed her hand and pulled her toward the door. "Wait! What about my coat?" Mandy said.

"You won't need it. The car is warm," he replied and yanked on her arm.

They got into the car and Graham took off. "Where are we going?" she asked.

"To the ranch. I finally figured out what Dad did with the cash he got from Jimbo."

"What?"

"I'm not going to tell you. I want to show you." He flashed her a boyish grin that reminded her of their childhood days.

"I'm definitely curious," she replied.

"You're going to be shocked in a good way," he replied.

For the next few minutes she tried to wheedle more information from him, but he refused to say anything more. "You've got me half crazy," she laughed.

"You're going to be full crazy when you see what I have to show you," he replied with a laugh of his own.

She sat up straighter in the seat as he turned in to the ranch's long driveway.

He didn't stop at the end of the driveway but rather drove onto the pastureland and headed toward the tree line, where she spied a silver car she didn't recognize.

"Who's that?" she asked.

"A friend of mine. Don't worry, Mandy, he's here to help us."

"Help us what?"

"You'll see." There was still a simmering excitement in Graham's voice.

As Graham drove closer to the other vehicle, a man opened the driver's door and stepped out. He was a big guy with a bald head that gleamed in the afternoon sunshine. He was clad in a pair of worn jeans and a black wool overcoat. Mandy had never seen him before.

Graham brought the car to a halt and the two of them got out. "Mandy, this is Guy Templeton. Guy, this is my sister, Mandy."

The two nodded to each other. She wrapped her arms around her body in an effort to stay warm and looked at her brother. "So, what's the big surprise? What did you want to show me?"

"You're standing on it," he replied.

She moved her feet and stared down with a frown. "Standing on what?"

"Oil, Mandy. This land is filthy rich in oil."

She stared at him in stunned surprise. "Really?"

Oil? What could this mean for the two of them? Her mind couldn't quite wrap around it.

Graham nodded. "Dad sent a money order for twenty-five hundred dollars to a man named Greg Michaels. Greg lives in Texas and specializes in building oil wells."

Her head spun as she tried to digest all this information. "Do you think this is why Dad was murdered? Why we've been attacked?"

"It's only part of it." Graham took a step closer to her.

"Dad was murdered because I wanted him dead." The glimmer in Graham's eyes turned to something dark and ugly as he held her gaze.

"I didn't run away from here, Mandy. I was only fourteen years old and he threw me out, and every day for all these years I dreamed of his death."

Mandy stared at him, her brain simply unable to process the horror of his words. "I—I don't understand. You—you killed him?"

"No," Graham scoffed. "I try not to get my hands dirty whenever possible. That's why I have my friend."

"I killed the old man," Guy said.

Confusion clouded her brain as she once again looked at her brother. "But—but you were beaten. Somebody attacked you."

A low rumble of laughter escaped him, a particularly unpleasant sound. "I told Guy just to rough me up a little bit. He was a little too enthusiastic."

Danger. Oh God, she was in danger. She didn't even have her phone with her. It was in the pocket of her coat at the café. "Why, Graham? Is the story about the oil really true?" Good grief, why was she asking about that when he'd just told her he was responsible for their father's death? It was as if her brain had just gone haywire.

"Damned straight it's true. I saw a report years ago…before that son of a bitch threw me out. I've been biding my time to take him out." Graham's face reddened as he continued.

"He kicked me to the curb and kept his precious daughter. You didn't ever have to worry where your next meal was coming from or where you were going to sleep for the night."

"But what about your foster family?" she asked.

"There was no foster family," he retorted angrily. "I scrabbled and stole to survive the streets. You were the golden child worth keeping and I was a big fat nothing."

"The golden child? You're out of your mind. He only kept me around so I could cook and clean for him. He abused me mentally and verbally every single day of my life. You were the lucky one. You got away from him." The words tumbled from Mandy's mouth at the same time alarm bells were ringing loudly in her head.

"I deserve this." Graham's eyes narrowed. "I deserve it all. I'm sick of working long hours and having to do what other people tell me to do. I'm going to be rich, and the only thing standing in my way now is you."

"Tell me this is some kind of a joke," she said desperately. "Please, Graham, don't do this." As Guy took a step toward her, she turned and ran.

The frigid wind sliced through her, but it was the sound of Guy's and Graham's malicious laughter just behind her that filled her soul with an icy terror.

She ran as fast as she could, cursing the heels of her shoes and the rough terrain. She wasn't fast enough. They were going to catch her and then what?

Death. It was now chasing her down in the form of a brother she had trusted. He'd been so devious, setting up alibis for himself, even going to the length of allowing himself to be beaten so that no suspicion would fall on him.

What had happened to him that had broken him so badly? Had her father really thrown him out of the house or had he run away? It didn't matter now. All that mattered at this moment was surviving.

Her lungs ached with her exertions and the cold, and more than once she threatened to lose her footing and stumble to the ground. If she could just get to the big house there was a lockbox on the door and she knew the combination.

She could get inside. The phone service hadn't

been shut off yet. She could call for help. She could call Brody. Oh, Brody! His name crashed over and over again in her head. Brody would save her if she could just get inside the house.

The hopeful thought barely had time to take full form when she was tackled from the back. Her elbows and knees hit the ground hard with one of the men on top of her.

Tears of pain and horror blurred her vision as Guy got off her and then roughly yanked her up and back to her feet. Her eyesight cleared enough to see Graham standing in front of her, a grin on his mouth.

"We haven't come this far to let you screw it all up," he said. "If somebody had done their job right the first two times you wouldn't even be an issue now."

"My bad," Guy replied with another one of his vile laughs.

"You won't get away with this," Mandy cried. "Daisy is expecting me back at the café. She knows you came and picked me up."

"And I kept my promise to her and dropped you off in front of the café. From there I have no idea what happened to you," Graham replied with a self-satisfied look on his face.

"Don't worry. I'm not going to kill you right away," Guy said as he tightened his hand around her upper arm.

"We have it all worked out," Graham continued.

"I'm leaving here now to head to the Watering Hole and Guy is going to wait three or four hours before he kills you. I'll have a solid alibi for your time of death and nobody knows anything about Guy."

Mandy stared at her flesh and blood, not believing how matter-of-factly he was talking about her murder. "You're insane," she said.

Graham laughed. "Yeah, maybe. But you'll be dead, the ranch comes to me and I'll get to enjoy the real riches of the land."

"Don't worry, I'll make sure to leave your body someplace where it will be discovered quickly," Guy said. "We don't want any wild animals to make the time of death harder to determine."

"Now I'm heading back into town," Graham said. "I trust you have all of this under control," he said to Guy.

"I've got you covered," Guy replied and then yanked on her arm. "Come on. I can at least keep you warm in the car before I slit your throat."

Graham walked back to his car as Guy dragged her toward his. Mandy would have screamed, but she knew there was nobody to hear her. The closest neighbor was Aaron, and even if he heard her scream she doubted he'd do anything to respond. Still, screams filled her head as Guy threw her in the passenger seat and slammed the door.

She waited until he'd left the side of the car and

then scrabbled for the car handle, intent to run again. Only there was no handle to open the door.

Her heart stopped. She was trapped with a killer and had only hours left to live.

"Heading out?" Sawyer asked as he met Brody at the barn door.

"Yeah, it's about that time." Brody pulled his coat collar more tightly around his neck and set his hat more firmly on his head. There was a cold wind blowing and a possibility of snow over the next couple of days.

"Tell Mandy hi for me," Sawyer said.

"Will do." Brody headed for his truck and minutes later was on his way into town and the café.

As he drove, his mind wandered, as it had for the past two days, to the night of their lovemaking. He'd been so adamant that it wouldn't happen again. But it had, and she'd been so eager, so passionate. That night the woman was indelibly etched into his heart. Into his very soul.

He could admit now that his physical desire for Mandy was beyond his control. It was a force of nature that he couldn't rein in.

It wasn't just a physical desire that plagued him. If he allowed himself, he could see a future with her. He could easily imagine waking next to her in bed and then sharing their morning coffee together. In the evenings with her, he wanted to sit and exchange the events of their days.

He wanted to lie next to her in bed each night and make love to her and then just listen to her breathe until he fell asleep.

Dammit, that night they'd gotten stranded at the motel, he'd never dreamed she'd become so important in his life after such a short period of time. He'd never thought that having a relationship with a woman could be so easy, so effortless.

There was no question about it—he would be a changed man when he walked away from her. Perhaps a bit bitter because he had experienced love and would never allow himself to experience it again. Of course, Mandy hadn't actually said she loved him, but he knew she did. He'd never experienced loving a woman before, but he knew he loved Mandy.

He would have wonderful memories of her...her joyful laughter, the smiles that warmed him from head to toe and the inner strength that was so admirable.

It was as if already his soul was dying a slow and painful death. He was grieving deeply for the loss of the future he chose not to have.

He tightened his hand around the steering wheel, hating himself for thoughts of love and Mandy. Dillon had believed the killer was getting desperate. Although Brody would never wish any harm to Mandy, he needed something to break that would put an end to the crazy relationship he'd found himself in.

Even as he thought about the need to end things with Mandy, his heart quickened with the anticipation of seeing her again in mere minutes. She'd twisted him up thoroughly in the head.

He found a parking space down the street from the café and then hurried toward the door, looking forward to getting in out of the brutal wind.

There were several couples seated at tables and booths and no sign of Daisy at the cash register. Mandy wasn't in the dining room, either, and he assumed she was in the kitchen.

He sat on one of the stools at the counter and released a deep sigh. He'd been heartsick since the night they had made love again because he wanted to do it again and again…

Somehow he had to be strong enough for the both of them. It was vital that he start distancing himself from her. There could be no more lovemaking. He had to go back to the man he'd been before he met her.

Daisy came around the corner from the kitchen and stopped in her tracks. "Mandy isn't with you?" she asked in surprise.

He looked at her in confusion. "Isn't she here working?"

"She was, but Graham came in here and stole her away. He said he'd have her back here within a half hour, but she didn't come back. I just assumed she was someplace with you."

Dread thundered in his heart and spread through his entire body. "What time was it when she left?"

"I think it was around two or so. Graham seemed real excited. Maybe something came up and she couldn't get away to come back to work," Daisy replied.

"Did he say where they were going?" He got to his feet.

Daisy shook her head and worried her hand through a strand of her bright red hair. "Do you think she's in some kind of trouble?"

"I don't know," Brody replied. "All I know is that I need to find her right now." He grabbed his cell phone and punched in her number. It rang three times and then went to her voice mail.

"Mandy, when you get this message, call me immediately." He hung up and didn't wait to say another word. He raced for the door, a frantic pounding in his head.

Graham. He'd been suspicious of the man initially, but between his alibis and his beating, Brody had been certain Graham was innocent.

How was it possible he was the source of the danger? He'd been at a Christmas party in Dallas when his father had been murdered. He had solid alibis for when the attacks had occurred on Mandy. Hell, he'd even been beaten up by somebody. The injuries he'd sustained certainly hadn't been self-inflicted. So, what in the hell was going on?

He got into his truck and pulled out his cell phone, trying to staunch the flood of fear that consumed him. He wished like hell he'd asked for Graham's phone number at some point in time, but it hadn't seemed important for him to have that number until this moment. He dialed Dillon's number, grateful when the man picked up on the first ring.

"Dillon, Mandy is missing," he said. "She disappeared from the café this afternoon with Graham and never came back."

"Where are you?" Dillon asked.

"I'm at the café. I'm going to head out to the ranch and see if they're there." God, he hoped they were there and she was okay.

"I'll check in town for them and get back to you. And Brody, try not to worry. We'll find them."

Try not to worry. Dillon's words rang in his head as he started his truck and headed for the ranch. There could be a perfectly logical and innocent reason that Mandy hadn't returned to the café.

If Graham had seemed excited, Brody hoped it had something to do with the house. Maybe Graham had found something they'd missed when packing everything up.

Graham knew the danger they were in. Wouldn't he do everything in his power to protect the sister he'd been reunited with? He appeared to adore her. Mandy was so easy to adore.

Still, even with these reassuring thoughts in his head, they didn't stop the frantic beat of his heart or the screech of alarms ringing inside his head.

He just needed answers as soon as possible. He drove fast, unmindful of the speed limit as he prayed they would be at the house and no harm had come to Mandy. It was the only place he knew to look, the only place that held something in common for both of them.

He pulled into the driveway and drove past the house to the detached garage.

Mandy's car was there, parked where it had been since he'd moved in. Graham's rental car was no place in sight. Brody turned off his truck and raced up the stairs to the apartment. The door was locked and he was fairly certain she wasn't inside, but he banged on the door anyway.

"Mandy?" He called her name and pounded on the door several more times to confirm to himself that she wasn't home. He then ran to the big house and knocked on the back door. *Answer...please, Mandy, answer the door.*

No response.

He hurried back to his truck and had just started the engine when his cell phone rang. It was Dillon.

"Graham is here at the Watering Hole. He says he dropped Mandy back at the café at about three."

Brody nearly dropped his phone at this news. It was his worst nightmare. Somebody wanted Mandy dead and now she was missing. "Did he see anyone else around? Did he see her go inside?"

"Negative on both counts. She got out of his car and he drove on."

"But she never made it inside the café." Brody's heart began to pound once again with a nauseating fear. "And I'm at the ranch and she isn't here. I've checked both her apartment and the house."

"I'll get all my men out looking for her. We'll find her, Brody."

"Thanks, Dillon." Brody hung up before emotion could completely overwhelm him. Oh God, where could she be? Was somebody holding her against her will? Had she been grabbed off the street or had she gotten into somebody's car willingly? And who would she have gone with willingly? Nobody. The answer echoed inside his head. She knew not to trust anyone.

What he feared more than anything else was that they were already too late to save her.

Chapter 14

It felt as if Mandy had been seated in the car waiting for death for forever. Guy had the audacity to try to visit with her, asking her about her Christmas holidays and if she'd made any plans for New Year's Eve.

He told her about growing up in Texas and that he loved to hunt and fish. He asked her what her hobbies were and if she liked pizza.

She didn't speak to him. She certainly didn't want to pleasantly chat with the man who intended to kill her. He was nothing but murdering scum and he didn't deserve a breath of conversation from her. The only person worse than Guy was her brother.

Her brother. Emotion squeezed her throat tight.

She'd been so happy to see Graham on the day of their father's funeral. It had been like a dream come true.

She'd been thrilled when they'd talked about a close and loving future together. They'd made plans for her to come to Texas and for him and his fiancée to visit her for the Fourth of July celebration.

Lies...all lies. He had hugged her and kissed her cheek. He'd eaten at her table on Christmas day and all the while he'd been plotting her death.

She'd never suspected his rage, his utter hatred of her and their father. She'd never suspected that he was behind the attacks, that he was so sick in the head he'd let Guy beat him to further his show of innocence.

It had been a devious and successful plan. Graham had made sure he had alibis for everything that had happened, and Guy had been a ghost in the night committing the crimes and getting away. She had no idea where he'd been staying, but she did know nobody in Bitterroot knew of his presence.

Her biggest regret was, she knew somehow Brody would believe this all happened because of some sort of failure on his part, when in fact she'd put herself in this position. She should have never left the café. She should have insisted that if Graham had something exciting to show her then he could just wait until after work when Brody was with her. Brody had warned her not to trust anyone and she'd definitely trusted the wrong person.

"Is it true what he said about the oil?" She finally broke her silence.

"According to Graham it's true, and he wouldn't have gone to all this trouble if it wasn't true. Although I can't for the life of me figure out why your old man did nothing about it for all these years," Guy replied.

Laziness, she thought bitterly. Laziness and drunkenness. Who knew why her father had waited so long to do something about the oil on the property? None of that mattered now. All that mattered was time was ticking by and it wouldn't be too long now before Guy killed her.

"I'm assuming Graham promised you something. Maybe you and I could cut some sort of a deal—a better deal—if you don't hurt me and let me go right now." She turned in the seat to look at her captor.

He grinned at her, exposing a missing eyetooth on one side of his mouth. "Your brother would hunt me down and kill me if I turned on him."

Mandy didn't miss a beat. "Then kill him first," she replied without blinking an eye.

Guy roared with laughter. "Aren't you the big bad girl now." Mandy's cheeks warmed at his obvious derision. "Your brother and I go way back and I'm not a double-crosser."

Her embarrassment gave way to a cold despair. "Could you turn on the heater again? I'm freezing."

"Sure thing," he replied. He started the car engine and within a matter of minutes warm air blew from the vents. But it couldn't begin to warm the iciness inside her.

Sheer panic rose up in the back of her throat. She had to do something to save herself. But what? She couldn't even get out the passenger door.

She shot a quick glance to the car door behind the driver seat. It had a handle. A small burst of adrenaline filled her, adrenaline combined with a hint of wild hope. If she could get to the back seat she could get out of the car.

Over the past couple of hours she'd desperately prayed for rescue, but time was ticking off for her and no rescue had come. She didn't believe anyone would find her. Even if Brody or the police went to the big house and her apartment, there would be no reason for anyone to look out to the wooded area of the pasture.

It wouldn't be long before the sun would start sinking in the sky. She wouldn't live to see the sunset and had to take a chance. She'd rather die fighting than just sitting and waiting for death to claim her.

Drawing several deep breaths, she steadied herself and then slid off her shoes. She could run faster without them. As Guy stared out the window and tapped his fingers on the steering wheel, she shot over the seat. Guy tried to stop her, but she managed to get to the back door and flew outside.

She ran without direction, wanting to find someplace to hide, someplace where Guy couldn't find her. She heard the slam of his car door.

"Damn you, girl," he shouted from behind her.

She didn't look back. She put her head down and ran for her life.

"Dammit, I should have waited to see that she got into the café okay," Graham said as he, Brody and Dillon stood just outside of the café. "I let her off right outside and assumed she'd be okay. Would she have gotten into another car of her free will? Maybe a girlfriend's?"

"Mandy doesn't have any friends. All she has is me," Brody said flatly. His heart hurt so badly he could scarcely get the words out.

They had all, along with Dillon's men, driven around town, checking out the suspects Dillon had, but they hadn't found her. Too much time had gone by now and a sense of despair nearly overwhelmed Brody.

He was lost. What could have happened to her? How had this happened and who was responsible? Jimbo had been at his pawn shop when Dillon had checked him out. His lackeys had been missing and Dillon had a couple of his men trying to find Sean Watters and Donny Pruitt.

Lloyd Green had been at the Humes ranch and Aaron Blair had been with his wife at the local pizza place at the time when Mandy had disappeared.

So, was Jimbo behind all this? Had his men picked Mandy up off the street? Were they just trying to scare her? As Brody thought about the ring of bruises around her neck, he knew he couldn't fool himself into pretending this was just a scare tactic.

"Why did you take her from the café in the first place?" Brody asked.

"I found a letter to us from our mother," Graham replied. "She'd written it when she knew she was dying."

"Why couldn't you have just brought it into the café?" Brody asked, his chest still so tight he could scarcely breathe.

"It was stuck on the floor in the master bedroom between the trim and the wall. If I tried to remove it, it would have ripped to shreds. I took her with me to read it because I knew it would do her good to hear how much our mother loved us."

Dillon's phone rang and Brody's heart leaped to life. Had somebody found her? He watched intently as Dillon listened to whoever had called.

"Okay, got it," Dillon said and then disconnected. "That was Ben. Sean and Donny were together at Donny's place and there was no sign of Mandy."

Brody stared at Dillon, the moment of hope seeping out of him. "If nobody on our suspect list has her, then who?" he asked desperately, even knowing nobody had the answer.

Their conversation was interrupted by several familiar pickup trucks pulling into parking spaces in front of the café. A lump formed in Brody's throat as Sawyer, Flint, Mac and Jerrod got out.

"We heard Mandy is missing and we're here to help," Sawyer said.

"The other men will be coming in a few minutes," Flint added.

Brody's brothers. The lump got bigger in the back of his throat.

They had come to help because that was who they were...a team who had always looked after each other. Since they had been young teenagers, they had always had each other's backs when bad times hit.

He listened while Dillon caught them up on what had happened and where they had already searched. As the Holiday Ranch cowboys scattered to continue the search, another howling wind of despair blew through Brody.

"What if whoever took her isn't even on our radar?" he said to Dillon. "What do we do next? Search every house in town? Besides, it's probably already too late."

"Don't say that," Graham replied. "It can't be too late." His eyes welled up with tears. "I already lost so many years with her. I refuse to believe that it's too late." He swiped at his eyes with the back of his arm.

Brody's tears were trapped inside him, making him feel half-nauseated. "I'm going to drive around again," he said, needing to do something...anything but stand here with his emotions growing to a point he could barely maintain control.

"Let's plan on checking back here in about an hour," Dillon said. "And in the meantime if you find her, call me immediately."

Brody got back into his truck and sat for a moment, the press of tears burning hot at his eyes. He'd called her phone over and over again and had been surprised when Daisy had answered it, letting him know it had been in Mandy's coat pocket in the café's break room. Wherever Mandy was, she didn't have her phone and she didn't have a coat.

As he headed down Main Street at a snail's pace, he didn't even know what he expected to see. It wasn't likely Mandy would be on the sidewalk walking without a care in the world. Nor would she drift out of a storefront and tell everyone she was just shopping the after-Christmas sales.

Mandy would never do anything to make him worry about her. He knew with a gut certainty she'd been somehow taken off the street, and who knew where her body would eventually be found?

Tears blurred his vision as grief grabbed him by the throat. Unable to see the road through the mist, he pulled over to the side as wracking sobs escaped him.

He hadn't wanted to pursue a long-term relationship with her because he wanted to keep her safe from any harm he might do to her. It was inconceivable to him that harm had found her anyway.

His shoulders shook with the force of his grief. He couldn't remember the last time he'd cried, but he was definitely not in control of the tears that escaped him now.

Giving into them, he leaned his head back and closed his eyes as he wept for Mandy. Although he'd intended to walk away from her, he wanted her to live and find that love she'd been searching for. He'd wanted her to find her prince and have the babies she'd wanted.

He couldn't stand the thought of not seeing her beautiful smile, of not having her in the world. It wasn't fair. Dammit, it just wasn't fair that she was the one targeted.

If he could, he would gladly change positions with her. He wasn't worth much to anyone and nobody would really miss him if he wasn't here. Mandy deserved her future of a husband and children, of love and laughter.

He finally leaned forward and swiped at his eyes as the tears began to subside. He didn't want to just sit here and waste time crying. His tears served no purpose. He needed to keep looking for her. Damn, but he needed to find her.

For the next half an hour he drove the streets of

Bitterroot, and then he headed back to her place on the desperate, improbable chance she might be there.

When he reached the detached garage, once again he raced up the stairs and banged on the door. Just as he expected, there was no answer.

Mandy... Mandy. His heart cried her name over and over again. He leaned against the door as his breath hitched painfully in his chest.

He finally pushed himself off the door and headed back down the stairs. It would soon be time to meet Dillon back at the café. He'd received no phone calls so it was apparent nobody had found her.

Starting back to his truck, his gaze swept the area. He froze in his tracks as the sun sparked off something metal in the distance.

Squinting his eyes, he focused in on the object. A car parked close to the woods. It was a silver car he'd never seen before.

Heart thudding in a new rhythm, he headed around the house where he could get a closer look and not be seen. His hand automatically reached for his gun and he moved in a crouched position.

Why would anyone be parked on this land? Who in the hell was in the car and what were they doing here? His heart slowed to a beat of cold determination.

He kept to the tree line at the side of the house and crept forward. He breathed through his nose, afraid that even a puff of frosty air might alert whoever was out there to his presence.

Closer and closer he got. Now he could see that the car appeared empty. What the hell?

A scream rent the air. Every muscle in his body tensed. Mandy! She was still alive. Then he saw her…being dragged by her hair out of the woods and toward the car by a burly bald guy he'd never seen before.

Whatever was happening, Brody needed to stop it right now. Afraid to shoot with the two of them so close together, instead he yelled to make his presence known.

"Hey," he shouted.

Mandy was thrown to the ground and it was only as the bald man attempted to get into the car that Brody fired his gun. He was an excellent shot, but the first shot hit the side of the vehicle.

He steadied his aim and fired again. The second one found its mark. The man screamed and fell to the ground, holding his knee.

Brody ran toward the man, who writhed in agony just outside the driver's door. The man tried to fight him off and cursed as Brody frisked him, retrieving a wicked-looking knife and the car keys.

"Brody," Mandy cried. She got up from the ground and ran to him. She slammed into him with a frantic force and shivered and cried.

He held her tighter than he'd ever held her before,

his heart beating wildly as she cried into the front of his coat. "It was Graham. He's behind everything. He's...he's a monster," she managed to weep.

"Are you hurt?" Brody asked. It was the only thing on his mind. He needed to make sure she hadn't been harmed. "Did he hurt you?"

She shook her head. "No...no, I'm okay." She looked at him, her face tear-streaked. "It was my brother, Brody. He drove me out here so that man could kill me. He...he was going to slit my throat."

Shock jolted through him. Graham? The man who had teared up only an hour before when he'd spoken about his beloved sister? "I need to call Dillon." Brody grabbed his cell phone from his pocket and then took off his coat and draped it around her shivering shoulders.

The man on the ground continued to curse, and then he gave Brody a sly smile. "I don't know what she's talking about. I wasn't going to hurt her. We're lovers and she contacted me and wanted to meet me out here. Go on, Mandy, confess. Tell him that we've been hooking up for the better part of a year."

"Shut up," Brody replied and punched in Dillon's number. He had no idea about the identity of the man he'd shot or what his relationship was to Graham. Mandy was alive and that was all that mattered.

"Dillon, I found her," he said into the phone when the lawman answered. "She's okay. We're out on the ranch in the pasture. There's a man out here with us.

I shot him and if you don't get your men out here quickly I'm going to beat the hell out of him, as well."

"On our way," Dillon replied.

Mandy continued to shiver and cry. "I can't believe you found me. I thought for sure I was going to die. He…he was going to kill me. He…he killed my father."

Once again Brody drew her closer to him as he glared at the man on the ground. "Graham made me do everything," he said. "He told me he'd kill me if I didn't carry out his orders." The man's voice took on a whining quality. "I didn't want to do it, but he made me. He's crazy."

"The victim card looks stupid on you," Brody replied.

"You didn't even ask for a damned ambulance," the man spat. "I could be bleeding to death."

"And neither of us will cry at your funeral." Brody guided Mandy farther from the car. There was no way the man was going to get away from here with a blown right knee and no car keys.

As they waited for Dillon to arrive, Mandy told him in choking sobs about the oil on the property, Graham's hatred and Guy doing the dirty work to make Graham appear innocent.

The sound of sirens was music to Brody's ears. Within minutes Dillon arrived along with an ambulance and four officers.

As Guy was loaded into the back of the ambulance, Mandy told Dillon everything she'd told Brody. "Where's Graham now?" Brody asked when she was finished.

"He called me and told me since he didn't know the town well, he'd be at the Watering Hole, waiting for news," Dillon replied.

"The news that my body had been found," Mandy said with a touch of bitterness. "Before you officially arrest him I want to see him." She turned and looked at Brody. "Take me to the Watering Hole?"

"With pleasure," he said grimly.

"You can both come with me," Dillon said. "Once Graham is arrested I need to get a full statement from Mandy at the police station."

Minutes later Brody and Mandy were in the back seat of Dillon's car and heading back into town. Officer Michael Goodall followed them in his patrol car.

Mandy had finally stopped crying, but she leaned weakly against Brody's side. She had to be exhausted. Besides being held against her will, she had the emotional trauma of believing she was going to be murdered. Hell, Brody was exhausted and he hadn't even been the one whose life was on the line.

As they reached Main Street, she sat up straighter, as if the idea of confronting her brother had given her a burst of adrenaline.

Now that she was safe, an anger brewed inside Brody. A white-hot rage that tightened his chest.

Damn Graham Wright for coming here with a killing mission. Damn him for his evil intent.

As Dillon pulled up in front of the Watering Hole, Brody tried to tamp down the rage, but it was wild and free inside him.

Mandy's eyes blazed with a fire he'd never seen there before. It was the flame of betrayal, of rich and righteous anger. When they stepped inside the dimly lit bar, he saw Graham seated on one of the stools at the counter.

The man was laughing, but the laughter halted abruptly when he saw them. His eyes widened slightly at the sight of his sister.

"Oh, thank God you found her," he said as he slid down from the stool. His gaze shot first right and then left, as if seeking escape.

Before Brody even knew what he was going to do, he stepped up to Graham and slammed him in the face with his fist. The force of the blow threw Graham backward and his nose spurted a stream of blood. Damn, but his fist meeting Graham's nose had felt good and had momentarily quieted the raging beast inside him.

"Are you going to allow this?" Graham asked in outrage as he held his nose and glared at Dillon.

"If he wouldn't have hit you, I would have. You're nothing but a creep. You can spend the rest of your life in prison thinking of me being filthy rich." Tears glittered in Mandy's eyes. "All I wanted was my brother back. I was so excited about building a relationship with you and all you wanted was me dead so you could get the ranch. You're a real jerk, Graham."

She turned away from him and into Brody's arms as Dillon handcuffed Graham and read him his rights. "It was all Guy's fault," Graham said. "He told me he'd kill me if I didn't cooperate with him."

"We've already heard that story from your friend, Guy," Brody said, his voice laced with disgust. "You two can blame each other all you want while you entertain each other behind bars."

"Officer Goodall, take this man and see that he's locked up," Dillon said.

"With pleasure," Michael replied.

"Come on. I'll drive you two to the office so I can get a full statement from Mandy," Dillon said.

For the first time since he'd heard that Mandy was missing, an overwhelming relief swept through Brody. She had survived, and hopefully in time she would be able to fully put this all behind her.

The danger was finally over and all he had to do now was leave her.

Chapter 15

It was almost midnight when Dillon, Brody and Mandy got into Dillon's car to head back to the apartment. Mandy had never been so exhausted. Her emotions had been all over the place since Graham had brought her out to meet her death.

She leaned against Brody as the car traveled through the night. She'd gone through a terror like she'd never experienced before, a depth of sorrow for the life she wouldn't get to live and the love she'd never be able to give.

Graham's twisted hatred of her, the horror of realizing he'd been behind their father's murder and the attacks on her, had broken her heart.

Going through it all again for Dillon had been utterly grueling. Remembering escaping the car and running for her life only to be caught once again by Guy, reliving the moment when she'd understood Graham wanted her dead—each and every moment had built up a weariness she knew only sleep without dreams and time could assuage.

They drove silently through the night's darkness, and it was only when they pulled up in front of the detached garage that a disheartening thought struck her.

It was truly over, but that meant it was time for Brody to go back to his ranch. There was no reason for him to stay with her anymore.

Dillon got out of the car with them. "Mandy, I'm so glad you got through this. I consider this one of my failures. Needless to say I took Graham off my suspect list way too soon."

"All's well that ends well, right?" She forced a smile to her lips. "Don't beat yourself up, Dillon. Graham fooled us all."

"He sure as hell fooled me," Brody said.

"All I know is I'm ready for sleep," Mandy said wearily.

"I'll just tell you both good night. If I have any other questions for you, I'll call." With a small wave, Dillon got into his car and pulled away.

"Brody, you aren't going to leave tonight, are you?" she asked before they started up the stairs.

Please not tonight. Not with the residual fear that still burned in her heart. She couldn't stand the thought of being alone.

"It's late. Tomorrow is soon enough for me to head back to the ranch," he replied.

Tomorrow. When he left the apartment would he also tell her he was done being with her? She couldn't let him go without telling him of her love. But tonight was not the time. She felt too fragile for that kind of conversation. Her heart had been bruised and battered enough for one day by Graham.

The first thing she wanted to do when they got inside was take a long, hot shower. She needed to wash the ugliness of the day off her. She needed to erase the feel of Guy tackling her and of him grabbing her arm. Her knees were sore as were her elbows from the tackle, but it could have been so much worse.

While she stood in the shower scrubbing herself, tears mingled with the water. They were the last residue of her fear and relief at being alive. The release felt good and left her even more ready for the healing power of sleep.

When she left the bathroom, the lights were out, the candles by her bed were lit and Brody was on the sofa. She wanted to ask him to sleep with her, to warm her with his body heat and to wrap her in his arms. But she was afraid he'd deny her and she was just too fragile to take the chance.

She crawled into bed and released a deep, tired

sigh. She turned over on her side and stared toward the sofa, barely able to see his features.

"Brody?"

"Yeah?"

"Thank you for finding me."

"You can thank the sunshine. If it hadn't reflected off Guy's car, I probably wouldn't have noticed it parked there."

"Yes, but I know you wouldn't have stopped searching for me until you found me...or my body," she replied.

There was a moment of silence. "Thank God that didn't happen," he finally said. "Now..."

"I know, it's late and you're about to tell me to go to sleep."

"Good night, Mandy."

"Good night, Brody."

She rolled to her back and stared up at the dancing candlelight on the ceiling. Her eyelids slowly drifted closed and the next time they opened, daylight drifted in through the windows.

She sat up and looked around. Brody was at the table, drinking coffee, and he lowered his cup and smiled at her. "Good morning," he said.

"Good morning," she replied. "What time is it?"

"Just after nine. How do you feel?"

"Pretty good." She got out of bed, grabbed a pair of jeans, a coral T-shirt she knew looked good on her and her underclothes and then headed for the bathroom to dress for the day. "I'll be out in just a few minutes," she said.

"Coffee is waiting for you."

It took her only minutes to dress and brush her teeth and her hair. She lingered over her makeup, putting on mascara and a little blush and then a light pink sheen over her lips.

Today was the day she was going to tell Brody Booth how very much she loved him, and she wanted to look her best. And today was the day Brody would have to tell her what he felt about her.

He truly was her prince, the man she'd been looking for all of her life. She'd dreamed of him since she was a child, cooking and cleaning for her father. It was like a fairy tale come true and she desperately hoped he finally confessed that he loved her as deeply as she did him.

When she left the bathroom she couldn't help but notice that his duffel bag was already packed and by the door. The sight of it shot a sharp pain through her heart. She ignored it, poured herself a cup of coffee and then joined him at the table.

"Heck of a night," he said.

"Tell me about it. At least I didn't have any nightmares. I slept like a baby. What about you?" She picked up her cup and eyed him over the rim as she took a sip.

"I slept very well," he replied. "So, do you believe this story about oil being on this land?"

She frowned thoughtfully. "I'm not sure what to believe. Graham said he saw paperwork about it before my dad kicked him out. I need to go through all the papers we got from Dad's bedroom and hire somebody who knows more about it than I do. I'll tell you one thing I've decided. Whether there is oil here or not, I've decided not to sell."

He looked at her in surprise. "I thought this place held nothing but bad memories for you."

"It's amazing the things you think about as you wait for a man to kill you. Yesterday while I was sitting in that car, I thought about the house and the past. You're right—the house holds very few good memories for me—but I want to change all that. I want to fill that house with all the love I remember from when my mother was alive. I want those old walls to rock with laughter and love and dreams." *And I want you there with me*, a voice whispered in the back of her head.

"I hope you do that, Mandy. I hope no ghosts ever haunt you and you find the happiness you deserve," he replied. "And now I should probably get going."

"Wait, you can't go yet. I mean, I haven't even finished drinking my coffee." She drew in a deep breath. "And I haven't had a chance to tell you how much I love you."

His eyes instantly shuttered and a nerve began to tick in his jawline. Not exactly the response she'd been hoping for. But she was going to speak her mind whether he wanted to hear it or not.

"I love you, Brody. I'm madly, desperately in love with you. You are the prince I've been waiting for. You're the man I want to live with in the house. I want to have your babies and live happily ever after with you." The words tumbled from her mouth.

She reached across the table and covered his hand with hers. "I know if you look in your heart you'll realize you love me, too. Tell me you love me, Brody. Please tell me you're in love with me."

He pulled his hand from hers. "It doesn't matter whether I love you or not. It doesn't change the fact that I'm not going to be a part of your future."

She stared at him in confusion. "So, you do love me."

He got up from the table and his eyes blazed with a sudden anger. "Okay, so I love you, Mandy. I love you more than I'll probably ever love another woman for the rest of my life."

She also rose from the table as joy filled her. He loved her. "Oh, Brody, I knew it. I just knew you were in love with me."

"But this is the end of anything between us." His jaw clinched tightly. "To be honest, I'm not even sure I can still be your friend."

She stared at him wordless as her heart began a frantic fluttering in her chest. "But why?" she finally managed to squeeze out.

"It doesn't matter why." He took two steps toward the door.

She quickly moved to stand between him and his duffel bag, a tinge of anger rising up inside her. "You can't just leave here without telling me why," she exclaimed. "I deserve at least that much from you."

Once again his jaw tightened and his lips thinned. If he thought he was going to walk out of here without telling her why they couldn't be together, then he had another think coming. She'd ride his back all the way to his truck to get an answer. She'd leap into the bed of his truck when he drove away.

He must have seen the determination on her face. He swiped a hand through his dark hair and heaved a huge sigh. "Mandy, I don't want to hurt you."

"You think this isn't hurting me?" she asked incredulously. "You're killing me right now."

He grimaced. "I know this hurts, but you'll get over me. This hurt is only temporary, but it would be worse in the long run if I stayed."

"Tell me why, Brody, or I swear I'll stalk you every day of your life until you make me understand what's going on in that head of yours."

He released another sigh. "I don't want to love you and then hurt you like my father hurt my mother. I've been seeing a psychologist—Ellie Miller—because I'm afraid I have a monster inside me and I never want you to see it."

She stared at his handsome, tortured features. "A monster? What are you talking about?"

"My anger," he said harshly.

"What anger?" She honestly had no idea what he was talking about.

"You saw it explode…you saw me smash Graham in the face. I refuse to take the chance that I'll be just like my father." His voice was laced with a pain so great it resonated inside her.

"Oh, Brody." She took a step toward him. "You will never be like your father. As far as you hitting Graham, I wanted to smash his face in… Does that make me a monster?"

She took another step forward. "A monster would have let me remain lifeless on the floor of the kissing booth. A monster would have shot Guy a hundred times after he was already on the ground instead of waiting for Dillon to arrive to arrest him. I don't know what mental loop is going off in your head, but you need to stop it. I couldn't love a monster. I trust you with my heart, my soul and my life. You are not an abusive man. You are not your father, Brody."

His gaze held hers, and in the dark depths she saw love and desire and need. He grabbed her and pulled her tight against him and his mouth crashed down to hers.

It was a kiss of unadulterated love. His arms roamed up and down her back as his tongue danced with hers. She leaned into him, her heart beating with his. In this single moment in time she felt that they were one.

He broke the kiss and grabbed her by the shoulders. He gently moved her aside and then reached down and grabbed his duffel bag. "Goodbye, Mandy."

She watched him in stunned surprise as he went out the door. She remained inert for only a moment and then she ran after him. "Brody!" she yelled as she stumbled down the stairs.

The ground was covered with a dusting of snow that had fallen in the night and the temperature was freezing, but she had the heat of anger inside her.

"How can you turn your back on our love?" she said as she came face-to-face with him at his driver's door. "We'd be so wonderful together." The burn of tears mortified her, but she was no longer in control of her emotions. "How can you tell me you love me and then leave me?"

He reached out and dragged a finger across her trembling lower lip. "Find a real prince, Mandy." He tossed his duffel bag into the back of the pickup.

"You're a fool, Brody." Tears began to trek down her cheeks and she angrily tried to brush them away. "Oh, wait, I must be the fool. I must be as stupid as my father always told me I was to fall in love with you."

He held her gaze for a long, shattering moment

and then turned and got into his truck. "You're a jerk, Brody Booth," she yelled.

Then he started the engine and drove away. She watched until she could no longer see the truck, and it was only then she realized how cold she was. It wasn't from the outside temperature, but rather an icy fist that clutched her heart.

He was gone.

Even though he'd told her they had no future together, she hadn't really believed him. She'd trusted in the love she'd felt each time he held her, when they laughed together and when they had made love.

Her tears came faster and faster as she hurried up the stairs and back inside. She threw herself across the bed as deep sobs choked her.

She'd thought Graham had devastated her heart when he'd betrayed her, but that pain had been nothing in comparison to the utter brokenness she felt at this moment. She knew Brody's heart and his soul. She knew there wasn't a monster inside him just waiting to be released. She'd seen his compassion and she knew his tenderness. He was a good man and deserved all the happiness he could get. She believed with all her heart that she was his happiness.

But she couldn't make him reach out for her. Even though he'd told her he loved her, she couldn't force him to stay with her.

It was over. It was done…the danger and the desire. She would never be the same again. Brody had taken with him a huge chunk of her heart, leaving her feeling more empty than she'd ever felt in her life.

Her tears finally stopped. She went into the bathroom to wash her face. Mascara slid down her cheeks and her lipstick was only a memory. The sight of herself made tears well up in her eyes once again.

Darn him for his stubborn belief. Darn him for the fear that had to reside inside him. And damn his father for everything he had been…everything Brody was not.

She sucked up the last of her tears. She'd told Brody that when she woke up each morning she always chose to be happy. Tomorrow it wasn't going to be that easy.

"Do you have to step all over me to get to the food?" Brody said to Sawyer as they stood in line for lunch.

"You've really been a cranky bear since you came back to the ranch," Sawyer replied. "Maybe you should just call her."

"I'm not calling anyone," he growled.

It had been four long days since he'd left Mandy's apartment, and the entire town was still talking about the crimes that had taken place.

More important, it had been four days of agony and confusion for Brody. He'd never known the kind of loneliness that now had taken up permanent residence inside him.

He thought about Mandy every minute of the day and dreamed about her at night. He missed her laughter, the way a tiny wrinkle danced in the center of her forehead when she frowned. And her smile. How he missed her smile.

"Maybe I wouldn't step all over you if you kept moving." Sawyer's voice snapped him out of his wistful thoughts.

"Sorry," he mumbled darkly and quickly served himself a helping of Cookie's seasoned fries. He moved on down the buffet line and added a big hamburger and a serving of baked beans to his plate, then found a place at the table next to Flint and Mac.

Sawyer and Clay sat across from him, and as the men began talking about ranch business, Brody's thoughts filled once again with Mandy.

He should have never confessed that he loved her out loud. It would have made things so much easier on her if he hadn't said those powerful words to her. And he definitely shouldn't have given her that last kiss…a kiss that had revealed his heart to her.

But he had, and he'd never forget the sight of her tears. It broke his heart that those tears had been caused by him. The other thing that broke his heart was that she'd told him she must be as stupid as her father had told her she was to fall in love with him.

She'd spent so much of her life believing she was stupid and worthless, playing a role as the bad girl in town to ease the pain she'd lived with so long.

Worst of all, he wanted her to be happy yet couldn't stand the idea of her being with another man. How selfish could he get?

The day unfolded like the three before. He tried to focus solely on his work, but his mind refused to cooperate and instead filled with visions of the woman he loved.

His head rang with the sound of her giggles as he'd chased her around the room with a finger full of frosting. He smelled her scent everywhere...in his lonely room at night and during his rides in the pasture. His body warmed when he thought of holding her close in his arms, stroking the length of her naked body and making love to her.

Dammit, why couldn't he get her out of his head? His own thoughts were bad enough, but why did everyone who'd seen her over the past couple of days feel the need to tell him?

Sawyer had come back from lunch the day before and had told Brody she looked sad, but she had told Sawyer that the For Sale sign in her yard had been taken down and she was working in the big house in preparation for moving in there.

Mac had run into her on the street and came back to tell Brody she'd looked sad but had asked him if he'd be willing to play his guitar at a house party she intended to throw in the spring.

Would she invite Brody to the party? Doubtful. She hadn't even tried to call him...and he'd waited for a call from her. He'd been perversely hoping for one of those before-bedtime calls that they'd shared before George's murder.

"You're nothing but a miserable bastard," Clay told him at dinner that evening.

"Either call Mandy and make up or go see a psychiatrist," Sawyer added with one of his usual easy grins.

"A psychiatrist would be easier for him," Clay continued. "Brody isn't afraid of a shrink, but one bubbly beautiful female has him quaking in his boots."

"Knock it off. It isn't funny," Brody replied.

"I'll tell you what is funny," Sawyer said. "Rumor has it that Leroy Atkinson was stark naked and somehow locked himself out of his house yesterday."

"Now that is funny," Flint said.

Leroy Atkinson was an older widower who was best known for his belief that aliens visited his ranch on a regular basis. That same rumor had it that his living room was covered in aluminum foil to keep alien beams from reaching him. Leroy was like an eccentric uncle to most of the town, and especially close to Dillon.

"Wait…I'm not done yet," Sawyer continued. "While he was standing on his front porch trying to figure out what to do, Sharon Watson drove up to deliver some groceries to him."

The men all laughed. "Wait…I'm not done yet,"

Sawyer said again. "According to the story, he grabbed up that fat old coon dog of his in an effort to hide his unmentionables. The dog barked and Leroy dropped him. Sharon set the grocery bags down and ran for her car."

"So, how did he get inside the house?" Flint asked.

"Sharon called Dillon, who has a key to the house. He drove out and rescued poor Leroy," Sawyer replied.

"So, all's well that ends well," Brody said and then realized he'd just echoed one of Mandy's favorite sayings. For the rest of the meal Brady brooded about the woman who was no longer in his life.

An hour after dinner Brody sat in his truck in front of Ellie's house. He'd had no appointment and his knocks on her door had gone unanswered. A glance in her garage showed her car was missing.

He couldn't imagine that she'd be gone long and so he sat and waited. He wasn't sure what he wanted from her. He just felt the need to talk to somebody.

He wanted to know when he would feel better. Although he knew she couldn't tell him, he'd like to know how long it would take before he forgot that he'd ever loved Mandy.

Minutes ticked by. It was almost an hour later when Ellie's car finally pulled into the driveway. Brody got out of his truck to greet her.

Her trunk popped open, displaying a handful

of grocery bags. "Ah, just in time to help an old woman," she said to him as she got out of the car.

"And I'm glad to do it," Brody replied. He grabbed the bags and followed her to the door.

"Did we have an appointment?" she asked as she unlocked the front door and allowed him to go in before her.

"No, we didn't. I was just hoping I could catch you for a short session."

"We can do that. We can chat while I put my groceries away." She first pointed to a chair at the kitchen table and then pulled out a box of ice cream Drumsticks and smiled at him. "An old woman's indulgence." She placed them in the freezer and then eyed him directly. "So, why are you here, Brody? Has something happened?"

Those simple questions unleashed him, and for the next fifteen minutes he told her everything that had transpired between him and Mandy.

When he was finished he felt naked and wrung out and more vulnerable than he could ever remember. "If I'm doing the right thing in walking away from Mandy, then why do I feel like everything is so wrong?"

"Your problem isn't about loving Mandy. It's about loving yourself, Brody. It's about recognizing that you were a frightened little boy who desperately wanted your abusive father to love you." Ellie leaned forward. "It's about growing up and recognizing you deserve to love and be loved."

She sat across from him at the table and shook her head. "Brody, you have shown enormous restraint under the worst of circumstances. That kind of restraint speaks to the truth of who you are at your very core."

Something clicked inside him and a weight lifted from his soul. He had carried a burden of fear with him since the moment he'd left his father's house. Even though Ellie had told him the same things for the past six months, at this moment her words finally unlocked his heart and opened his eyes to real possibilities...including the possibility of a future with Mandy.

"I've got to go," he said and stood.

"Of course you do," Ellie replied with another smile. "Believe in yourself, Brody, and go and claim your woman."

With a nod, he raced for the door, suddenly... urgently needing to see Mandy. It wasn't until he got into his truck that new doubts crept in.

It had been four days. Was it possible he'd waited too long? Left her too cruelly for her to ever forgive him? Was it possible that in the four days they had been apart, she'd decided she didn't want him anymore? That he wasn't her prince?

Tension tightened his chest and his breaths became painful. What if it was too late? Dammit, he did deserve to love and be loved. He was a good man and he'd be a better man with Mandy by his side.

Twilight shadows drifted down as he drove to her ranch. She had to want him still, because he couldn't imagine his future without her. His heart banged against his ribs as he turned down the long drive.

The big house was dark and her car wasn't there, nor was her car parked in front of the garage apartment. The café! He slammed his truck into Reverse and took off back to town.

He felt as if he might explode if he didn't talk to her right now. His love for her was the only beast inside him and it begged to be set fully free.

He whirled into a parking space down the street from the café and got out of the truck. Doubts once again struck him, stopping him in his tracks.

Had he blown it forever with her? Would she find it in her heart to forgive him? He thought about what she'd told him—that each morning she always chose to be happy. For far too long he'd gotten up each morning and had chosen to be miserable.

Mandy had taught him a new way of thinking. She'd shown him what was possible. And it was with those possibilities filling his head that he settled his cowboy hat firmly on his head and then marched into the café with a determined stride.

If she would just give him another chance he would wake up each morning and choose love and happiness every day. He would do everything in his power to make sure that she had only happy days for the rest of her life.

He walked into the café and instantly saw her. She was waiting on a booth of people, and when she saw him her bright smile faltered. That scared him.

He sat at a table in her section, his heart once again beating so quickly he felt half-dizzy. She moved from one booth to the next and then finally approached his table.

"What can I get for you?" Her voice was cool and there was no smile for him.

"Mandy...we need to talk," he said. He removed his hat and placed it on the chair next to him.

"I heard everything I needed to hear from you," she replied. "So, what can I get you?"

Her eyes didn't quite meet his. He reached out for her hand, but she stepped back from him. His heart cracked. "Please, Mandy...just hear me out."

"Not now." She finally looked at him but her eyes were as cold as the wind outside. *Too late.* The words whispered through his mind. She released a small sigh. "I get off in two hours. I can give you a minute or two after that." She didn't wait for his reply but turned on her heel and stalked away.

Chapter 16

Mandy escaped into the kitchen, her heart quivering like a captured bird. She hadn't expected to see him here. She hadn't been prepared to see his handsome face tonight. She had hoped he'd have the decency not to come into the café during the hours she worked for at least longer than a mere four days.

Four days had certainly not given her time to heal from his rejection of her and her love for him. Heck, she was still crying over him when she was in bed at night.

New Year's Eve had come and gone and she'd spent the night watching happy people celebrate on television while she was eating chocolate cupcakes and crying.

It wasn't like she didn't think she could survive without him. She was stronger than that and she would survive just fine. But oh, she'd wanted him so badly.

Still, just because he'd shown up here and wanted to talk to her didn't mean anything had changed between them. She'd bared her heart to him once and he'd trampled on it as he hurried out of the door.

She'd been completely open and vulnerable and she wasn't likely to be that way with him again anytime soon.

"Should I kick him out?" Daisy asked when the two women met in the kitchen. "He's taking up table space and hasn't ordered a thing."

Mandy knew Daisy didn't give a darn about whether Brody ordered something or not. She was just letting Mandy know she had her back if Mandy needed it.

"No, it's okay. I'll serve him a piece of pie and a cup of coffee and demand a fifty-percent tip." Mandy attempted a teasing smile, but it fell flat. "He wants to talk to me. I told him we could talk after I got off work."

"What do you think he wants to talk to you about?" Daisy asked.

"I have no idea." Mandy couldn't help the small flicker of hope that lit up inside her.

"Don't let foolish pride screw you up," Daisy replied. "I made that mistake with my second husband." She frowned. "Or maybe it was my third. Anyway, pride rarely does anyone any good when it comes to matters of the heart. Now, get out of here and tend to the last of your customers."

Mandy's shoulders stiffened with tension as she grabbed a piece of apple pie and a cup of coffee and approached Brody once again. "Here you go," she said as she served him.

"Do I get service with one of your smiles?" he asked softly.

She forced a tight smile to her lips. "There, that's as good as they get these days." Once again she escaped his table as quickly as possible.

If he really needed to talk to her, why not the afternoon after he'd left her? Why not the day after? Why had he waited four agonizing days?

Why was he here? He'd already told her he loved her and had still left her. What more could there be to say between them? The questions and his presence had her on edge while she tended to her customers and her shift drew to an end.

She finished up and went into the break room to take off her apron and retrieve her coat. Her heart thundered wildly as she left the room to see Brody on his feet and standing by the front door.

"Bye, Daisy. See you tomorrow," she said.

"Good night, hon," Daisy replied.

"We can talk in my truck," Brody said as they

stepped out into the cold night air. Not a star or the moon was visible overhead.

"We can talk right here," she countered. She didn't want to sit in the truck that smelled of him, a fragrance that would only break her heart all over again.

It was better they talk here, where the only scents in the air were delicious aromas from the café and the faint smell of impending snow.

"So, what do you want to discuss?" She stared at his face in the light that came out of the café windows.

He stared back at her, his dark eyes filled with emotions she couldn't begin to discern. "First of all, I want to talk about me," he said.

Really? He'd broken her heart and now had pulled her out into a wintry night to talk about him and not them? Was he intentionally trying to torture her?

"Mandy, I love me." The words seemed to explode from him.

"Then I hope the two of you will be very happy," she replied.

Even in the dim lighting, she could see a deep red filling his cheeks. "That's not the way I mean to say it. I... I need to start over. Mandy, I've been afraid for years that I would become the brutal abuser that my father was. My belief got so bad a couple of months ago, I started seeing Ellie Miller."

"That's good, Brody. I admire that you sought help." With each of her words the tiny flicker of hope that had filled her dimmed. Was this what he'd wanted to tell her? That he was getting help for himself?

"I went to see Ellie this evening and something clicked inside me. I realized I need to love myself before I could love us." He took her by the shoulders, the emotion shining from his eyes one she recognized, and the flame of hope inside her burned brighter.

"I am a good man, Mandy. I will never be like my father. It's not in me. I'm a good man and I deserve to love and be loved. I deserve happiness."

"And now you love you?" she asked, her heart swelling in her chest.

He nodded. "And I love you, Mandy. If you'll give me a second chance I will never, ever leave you again."

"You have to be sure, Brody. You have to be very sure," she replied, her voice holding a tremor. "I don't want you to break my heart again."

"I'll never break your heart again," he replied with a fierceness. "I love you and I want to marry you. I want you to have my babies and to fill that old house with love and laughter. I am your prince, Mandy. Please tell me it isn't too late for us."

Joy exploded inside her. "Oh, Brody, it's not too late." She raised her arms around his neck and leaned into him. "You're right. You're the prince I've been waiting for all my life."

"And you're my princess."

Before she could say anything else his lips were on hers, speaking of his love for her in the warmth of his mouth against hers, in the arms that held her so tightly against him.

A happiness she'd never felt before filled her heart and soul. The knowledge that she was where she belonged shot a wonderful sense of peace through her.

When they finally broke the kiss it had begun to snow, which was fitting. They had first found each other during a snowstorm and now they'd sealed their love with a kiss while a gentle snow fell.

"Let's go home," he said, his eyes shining with the same kind of happiness that warmed her heart. "Ride with me and I'll bring you to pick up your car in the morning. Now that I have you I don't want to lose a minute of our time together tonight."

Oh, this cowboy took her breath away and she knew he would continue to take her breath away for many years to come. He was her best friend and her lover, and hopefully soon he would be her husband.

Brody stood at the front door of the big house, now home, and stared out at the empty driveway. Before long, cars would be arriving as friends attended the official housewarming party.

Mandy was in the kitchen, fixing all kinds of fancy finger food for people to enjoy. She had banished him from that room an hour ago, telling him he'd just get underfoot.

He smiled. He'd been doing that a lot since the night almost two months ago that he'd driven to the café with his love for her burning in his heart.

It was amazing to realize all he had to do to be truly happy was to claim a love of himself. He'd moved past his old memories instead of wallowing in them. He'd recognized on both an intellectual and an emotional level that the sins of the father were just that.

The past two months had been busy ones as they tackled getting the house ready for them to move in. Walls had been painted and furniture had been bought. Oak floors had been sanded and refinished and new curtains hung at all the windows.

They had decided George's old bedroom would make a great playroom for the children they hoped to have one day. They'd taken the largest bedroom upstairs as their master, and it was in the decorating of that room that they'd had their first fight as an official couple. He'd insisted there be no pink.

He smiled again as he remembered telling her no self-respecting cowboy would sleep under a black-and-pink bedspread. They'd finally compromised on a black spread with coral-colored throw pillows and coral curtains at the windows. The pink was now in one of the guest bedrooms.

He'd told Cassie he would continue to act as foreman for the time being, but eventually he'd be ranching this property and no longer working for her. She'd been happy for him and Mandy.

He'd also introduced Mandy to Ellie. The two women had hit it off, and he and Mandy were now considering asking Ellie to be a witness at the small, private wedding they were planning.

He straightened as he saw several familiar pickup trucks driving down the lane toward the house. The Holiday cowboys would be here in force to help celebrate.

He left the window and hurried into the kitchen, where Mandy was taking cheese-and-crab-stuffed mushrooms from the oven.

"We're about to be invaded," he said.

As she set the mushrooms down he grabbed her from behind and nuzzled her neck. "Stop," she said with a laugh and swatted at him with a pot holder. "Quick, help me get these on the server platter and on the table."

"Turn around and give me just a minute," he said.

"Okay, but just one minute." She turned to face him. Her cheeks were flushed and the red blouse she wore emphasized the rich darkness of her hair and her caramel eyes.

As always, the sight of her filled him with hot desire and tender love. "Mandy, we've been through a lot together and we've come out on the other side. We've fixed up this old house and managed to get through it with a minimum of fussing, but there's one thing I haven't done."

He pulled a ring box from his pocket and dropped to one knee. Her eyes opened wide and then began to mist with what he knew were happy tears.

"Mandy Wright, will you wear this ring and marry me and be my girl forever?" He opened up the ring box to reveal a beautiful one-karat round diamond with smaller gems on either side.

"Yes, you know my answer is yes," she replied breathlessly. "Oh, Brody, it's so beautiful."

He stood, took the ring out of the box and then slid it onto her finger. "I wanted a ring fit for a princess," he said.

She held her hand up in the air, gazed at the sparkling ring and then threw her arms around his neck. "I love you, Brody Booth."

"And I love you. It took us a while to get here, but all's well that ends well, right?" He gazed at her teasingly.

She laughed and then they were kissing and the doorbell was ringing. Brody knew the night would be filled with celebration and friends, and best of all was the sweet knowledge that he was finally home.

* * * * *

MILLS & BOON®

INTRIGUE
Romantic Suspense

A SEDUCTIVE COMBINATION OF DANGER AND DESIRE

A sneak peek at next month's titles...

In stores from 7th September 2017:

- **Rough Rider** – B.J. Daniels *and*
  Pine Lake – Amanda Stevens
- **Point Blank SEAL** – Carol Ericson *and*
  Texas Showdown – Barb Han
- **Mr Serious** – Danica Winters *and*
  Stone Cold Christmas Ranger – Nicole Helm

Romantic Suspense

- **Mission: Colton Justice** – Jennifer Morey
- **The Agent's Covert Affair** – Karen Anders

Just can't wait?
Buy our books online before they hit the shops!
www.millsandboon.co.uk

Also available as eBooks.

MILLS & BOON®

Why shop at millsandboon.co.uk?

Each year, thousands of romance readers
find their perfect read at millsandboon.co.uk.
That's because we're passionate about
bringing you the very best romantic fiction.
Here are some of the advantages of
shopping at www.millsandboon.co.uk:

* **Get new books first**—you'll be able to buy
  your favourite books one month before they
  hit the shops

* **Get exclusive discounts**—you'll also be
  able to buy our specially created monthly
  collections, with up to 50% off the RRP

* **Find your favourite authors**—latest news,
  interviews and new releases for all your
  favourite authors and series on our website,
  plus ideas for what to try next

* **Join in**—once you've bought your favourite
  books, don't forget to register with us to rate,
  review and join in the discussions

Visit **www.millsandboon.co.uk**
for all this and more today!

Join Britain's BIGGEST Romance Book Club

50% OFF your first parcel

- **EXCLUSIVE offers every month**
- **FREE delivery direct to your door**
- **NEVER MISS a title**
- **EARN Bonus Book points**

Call Customer Services

0844 844 1358*

or visit

millsandboon.co.uk/subscription

* This call will cost you 7 pence per minute plus your phone company's price per minute access charge.